celg

EXPEDITION DEEP OCEAN

Center Point
Large Print

**This Large Print Book carries the
Seal of Approval of N.A.V.H.**

EXPEDITION DEEP OCEAN

THE FIRST DESCENT TO THE BOTTOM OF ALL FIVE OF THE WORLD'S OCEANS

JOSH YOUNG

CENTER POINT LARGE PRINT
THORNDIKE, MAINE

For Samuel Macy Harrell III
and
In memory of Sally Bowers Harrell
with eternal gratitude

EXPEDITION
DEEP OCEAN

Knowledge of the oceans is more than a matter of curiosity. Our very survival may hinge upon it.

—**President John F. Kennedy, March 1961**

CONTENTS

PROLOGUE
SPACE TO SEA

Space, that final frontier, has long been the ultimate in exploration. In the early 1960s, a space race between the United States and the Soviet Union shifted into high gear. Space travel captured imaginations around the world. Sending humans into the heavens in a rocket and allowing them to look back at Earth was a romantic notion. And then there was the burning question of whether or not there was any life on the Moon.

Three major space programs funded by the U.S. Congress were launched by NASA with varying goals and results. Project Mercury, which began in 1958, was the first human spaceflight program administered by NASA. The program's goal was to put an astronaut into orbit around the Earth. With millions following the developments on radio, that goal was achieved by John Glenn on February 20, 1962, and he became a modern-day hero.

Project Gemini, which ran from 1961 through 1966, took the next step toward landing a man on the Moon. In a capsule built for two astronauts, the Gemini spacecraft flew low orbit missions that were working to perfect Mercury's orbital techniques and prove the feasibility of in-orbit docking, necessary to complete a Moon landing. But the human cost was high, as three astronauts lost their lives during Gemini training. Adding the loss of life to the financial cost, a vigorous debate began over whether space travel was actually necessary or more of a quixotic pursuit.

NASA pushed ahead. The Apollo program was the final step in landing a man on the Moon. The spaceflight program, through many travails and the loss of yet three more lives in Apollo 1, achieved its goal. On July 20, 1969, with the world at a virtual standstill as hundreds of millions watched on television, Neil Armstrong and Buzz Aldrin landed Apollo 11's lunar module, the *Eagle*, on the Moon. Later that day, Armstrong became the first human to walk on the lunar surface.

Each of the space exploration programs built on the previous one, and one could not have been possible without its predecessor. To reach the Moon through these three monumental programs, which adjusted for inflation cost more than $175 billion, there were incremental steps toward the completion of the full mission. The spacecraft had to launch, dock in orbit, and the astronauts had to then land the *Eagle* on the surface of the Moon. Finally, the astronauts needed to return safely to Earth. For all the money, engineering know-how, and technology, the core mission of the programs was fairly straightforward: to safely land a man on the Moon, take a soil sample, and return it to Earth for further study.

As a result of the space race and the continuing fascination with the Moon, 533 people have orbited Earth, and 12 have walked on the Moon. As a species collectively, including the Soviet Union's early missions, we've gone "up" into space with great success. But what about going "down" to the bottom of our oceans? What has come of the "oceans race?"

The answer is next to nothing, because there isn't really one.

Oceans cover some 70 percent of the planet's surface, driving weather, regulating temperature, and ultimately supporting all living organisms; and oceans have also been a vital source of sustenance, transport, commerce, growth, and inspiration, yet humans have explored only 20 percent of this virtual lifeblood. Most people struggle to even *name* all five of the oceans on our planet. Nothing has been more taken for granted—and more feared—than the deepest waters of the world.

The best known oceans, certainly to Americans, are the two that border the continental United States, the Atlantic Ocean to the east and the Pacific Ocean to the west. The largest and deepest ocean of them all, the Pacific Ocean covers some 63 million square miles and touches more than 40 countries and 23 additional territories, stretching across the curves of the globe from the United States to Australia to Thailand.

Further north and east of the Atlantic, past Greenland and continuing to the northern tip of Russia, is the Arctic Ocean, generally identified because of its relationship to the Arctic Circle and renowned for its cold waters and polar ice caps. The Indian Ocean stretches from Asia at the north, to Africa on the west and Australia on the east, and skirts Antarctica to the south. Its warmer temperature cannot support as much sea life as the other oceans.

The most difficult one to name, for most, is the lesser traveled Southern Ocean, which wraps around Antarctica and is usually defined as all the water south of 60 degrees south latitude—known by mariners as the "screaming sixties" because of its common, and ferocious, storms. It's the place of nature documentaries that feature the seals and whales of the Antarctic coastline and the penguins inhabiting the remote South Sandwich Islands far to the east of South America.

Despite the vital connection between the oceans and mankind, as of the turn of the calendar to 2018, only three people on two separate missions had been to the bottom of the Mariana Trench in the Pacific Ocean. Named the Challenger Deep, it has long been believed to be the deepest point of our five oceans at somewhere close to 10,916 meters, which is more than 35,000 feet, or roughly 6.7 miles.

The first mission to accomplish the dive was the U.S. Navy's Project Nekton on January 23, 1960, something of an oceanic Mercury mission with the goal being to reach the bottom. The submersible *Trieste* was piloted by Swiss engineer Jacques Piccard and U.S. Navy lieutenant Don Walsh, *Trieste*'s commander. It proved with brute force that a massive steel sphere, made buoyant by huge tanks that were filled with gasoline that was lighter than water, could reach the bottom of the Challenger Deep.

The second mission occurred on March 26, 2012, when filmmaker James Cameron piloted his single-person, steel-capsuled *Deepsea Challenger* submersible to the bottom. His mission took the next step and showed that not only could we reach the bottom in a manned submersible, but we could take the next step and remain there and explore for hours, making it the Gemini version of deep ocean exploration that built on what the *Trieste* had accomplished.

Those two missions were more than a half-century apart, a stunning commentary on the lack of curiosity about the deepest point on our planet. And no one had even attempted to reach the bottom of the other four oceans, and therefore no one knows what, if anything, of meaning might be there. The fact is that scientists don't fundamentally understand how the oceans interact with the atmosphere or even each other, because we don't have much reliable data—perhaps because 90 percent lies below 1,000 meters. Below 1,000 meters, the water pressure is over 1,400 pounds per square inch and marine engineers say that at that point, "things get really complicated." This depth is also generally referred to as the "crush depth" of most modern military submarines, and any craft capable of going below that depth requires special engineering, construction, and testing.

In 2018, a group set out to build a new machine that could go not just beyond 1,000 meters, but to 11,000, and—finally—dive to the bottom of all the world's oceans, a hoped-for Apollo-like deep ocean mission. To accomplish this, a 46,000-nautical-mile expedition, wrapping around the globe and then some, was set in motion and financed by a ponytailed Texan with a penchant for exploration that had led him to the peak of the highest mountain on each of our seven continents and to ski both poles, completing the so-called Explorers' Grand Slam.

A self-proclaimed loner, polymath, and sci-fi junkie, the private equity investor risked a sizeable portion of his net worth to finance the project and attempt to become the first human to reach the bottom of all five oceans, video the ocean floor, and return with sediment and sea life samples.

The submersible to take him to the depths was designed by a Briton who has never read a book on subs and doesn't believe in formal engineering training as a means of building them. Instead, he relied on a vision of what was possible based on a combination of his imagination and a study of the physical properties of the components. The submersible was built by the Brit's employer, a Florida-based company owned by two partners, one a somewhat combative former gemologist, the other a gregarious Canadian who drops an f-bomb with flair in every third sentence. Certification would need to come from a narrow-focused German expert who knew as much, or more, about submersibles than any of the other principals.

The expedition leader was a former New Zealand park ranger living in Seattle whose firm specializes in exotic sea expeditions and was once the subject of a "Modern Love" column in the *New York Times* in which his wife wrote, "My father warned me about guys like you." The science portion of the mission was slotted to be led by a speaks-his-mind Scot from Newcastle University on his 55th oceanic expedition who had literally written the book on the Hadal Zone—all depths deeper than 6,000 meters—called, quite appropriately, *The Hadal Zone*.

The ship, flying under a Marshall Islands flag to avoid unwanted complexities associated with flying a U.S. flag, was captained by another jovial, but highly professional Scot who earned his sea legs in the oil and gas business, and run by his fellow European engineers and a rotating crew of Filipinos with an Austrian doing the cooking. The entire expedition was filmed for not one but two television events, which were to be produced by an Emmy award–winning documentary film producer known for his ability to produce amazing footage and landmark non-fiction films, but who maintained such a tight grip on all media relating to the expedition that it frequently led to clashes with other team members.

This is the story of how they came together on the first expedition to ever attempt to dive to the bottom of the five oceans, in hopes of creating a marine system capable of reliably, safely, and repeatedly journeying to any point on the bottom of the ocean. Such a thing had never existed before in human history and they were determined to change that.

CHAPTER 1
THE EXPLORATION GENE

On a typically sticky late May evening in 2014, Victor Vescovo guided his Tesla through light traffic in his hometown of Dallas. He was on his way to one of his regular dinners with his older sister, Victoria. His mind was whirring, as his latest voyage of exploration was taking shape. He had been poking around the Internet for weeks, doing research, and was ready to put his new, somewhat radical idea in motion.

Tall and lanky, Vescovo is a native Texan, though he doesn't look much like one. His long face and gray beard are reminiscent of a centuries-old Italian painter. He has graying blond hair that he wears in a ponytail more indicative of a sculptor than a 49-year-old partner in a private equity firm.

The minute Vescovo sat down at a local favorite restaurant in her town of Coppell, ironically named Victor's Wood Grill, his sister knew something was up. The two are close even beyond being on the same page, or finishing each other's sentences. They're on the same wavelength, *and* amplitude.

Once when they were playing Pictionary,

Vescovo looked intently at his sister while drawing a single line, perfectly straight and rapidly, like it was shot out of a gun. From his expression and the *way* he drew it, she immediately shouted out, "Laser." It was the right answer, of course, and they weren't ever allowed to be on the same team again.

That night at dinner, she saw that determined, focused look in his eyes that she had seen so many times. When they were children, she had watched him build space capsules out of large cardboard boxes. He would "wire" the capsule to the family car with a household extension cord for power, and outfit it with a communications apparatus made from an old rotary dial telephone. He would then spend hours piloting his "craft" through space, using accurate commands and terminology from books he had read. Remarkably, he also built a working radio from a Radio Shack kit at age eight, and then a computer with cassette-tape-based storage when he was thirteen.

As an adult, Vescovo took his adventurous spirit to new heights, literally, and cemented his place among the elite mountain climbers of the world. He climbed the tallest mountain on each continent, thus being one of the 350 people to complete one of the ultimate climbing challenges known as the "seven summits." All the while, he was on his way to becoming a licensed helicopter pilot and later acquired a fixed-wing jet rating, eventually purchasing both a helicopter and jet so he could fly them himself.

"I've got this new thing I want to do," he said to Victoria. "Going to the bottom of all five oceans. I've researched it and I think the technology is there to build a sub that can make it. I even have a rough idea of the logo"—pausing, he gestured with his right hand—"pen?"

Victoria reached into her purse and pulled out a doctor's appointment card and a pen. A thin, elegant woman with straight silver hair, her distinguishing feature in public that night was a neck brace, which she covered with a scarf. In 2006, she had fallen while rollerblading and broken her neck. After five surgeries and the placement of titanium rods, she was still left with a lifetime of recurrent pain. The two of them together also carried a much deeper pain, the death of their sister, Valerie, who had committed suicide in 2002.

Vescovo sketched the outline of a badge on the card. Inside the badge, he drew five jagged, vertical lines in the shape of repeating V's. The troughs of the V's represented the bottom points of the five oceans, Atlantic, Pacific, Arctic, Indian, and Southern.

"So the seven summits and now the five deeps," he said. "It's almost symmetrical, right? I'm going to try and go to the bottom of the five oceans. Nobody has ever done it."

•   •   •

Victor Lance Vescovo has a unique perspective on life, one that he has defined himself rather than letting others define for him. Like most people, part of it comes from how and where he grew up, the experiences of his youth, and the more formative ones as an adult. Much of it though comes from his internal life, the time he has spent wrapped up in science fiction novels, a massive number of history books, and studying and playing military simulations.

Born in Dallas in February 1966, Vescovo is youngest of three children and only son to an Italian-American father, John Peter Vescovo from Memphis, Tennessee, and a German-Irish mother, Barbara Frances Lance (hence his middle name) from Waycross, Georgia. His father worked for Columbia Records, and the family moved around in Vescovo's early years, from New Canaan, Connecticut, to Silver Spring, Maryland. Living in the northeast erased any trace of a Texas drawl.

As a child, he was voracious reader and an avid fan of science fiction. Jules Verne's novels and *Star Trek* were early favorites. In his teens, he discovered Frank Herbert's landmark epic *Dune*, Isaac Asimov's *Robot* and *Foundation* series, the cyberpunk works of William Gibson, and David Brin's aqua-themed *Startide Rising*. Vescovo also discovered Iain Banks's genre-breaking Culture series in 2010. With ten books, the series was like the gift that kept on giving for him.

"I read everything I could get my hands on as a child and during my school years," he says. "I would actually just sit and read the encyclopedia—that was fun for me. I wanted to see the world, understand it, and do interesting things. And don't even get me started on maps. I could stare at maps for hours."

Intellectually, he was advanced. Some early IQ testing in grade school showed that he was off the charts, and school administrators told his parents that he needed to be suitably challenged. He was eventually enrolled in St. Mark's School of Texas, an all-boys prep school in Dallas. Reserved and introverted, he loved chess, military war games, and Dungeons & Dragons, and was a voracious reader of military history. He discovered books about exploration and eventually learned that Dick Bass, a St. Mark's alum, had summited each of the highest mountains on the seven continents. This planted a seed in his mind that perhaps, if his body and skill permitted it, he might be able to replicate the feat.

He attended college at Stanford University. His freshman year, he learned to fly a small Cessna, and a love of aviation was born. Known by his family and friends as Lance throughout his childhood, when he graduated from Stanford and started his first job in San Francisco, he asked his friends and family to start calling him by his first name, Victor.

"Victor had more gravitas than Lance," his childhood friend Matt Lipton says. "I think the change said to him that he wanted to be taken seriously."

At the time, he was considering going into the military. He had discussed this with his Stanford foreign policy professor, Condoleezza Rice, who later became president of the university and then national security adviser and secretary of state under President George W. Bush. She encouraged him to consider becoming a reservist while continuing on his business career—since it was obvious he loved both potential careers—advice that he eventually acted on.

Taking just three years to finish his undergraduate work, he graduated from Stanford in 1987 with a double major in political science and economics, with distinction. By his own admission, he did nothing but study, fly, and practice martial arts during his college years. Developing a social life held little interest for him.

Over the next dozen years, his life was dominated by three pursuits: a varied work life, serving in the Navy Reserve, and climbing the highest mountains.

Before Vescovo started his first job, at Bain & Company in San Francisco, the 21-year-old traveled to Africa with money he had saved up from trading stocks on the side. He ended up in northern Tanzania at the base of Mount Kilimanjaro. Upon seeing it, the only thought that occurred to him was: "Oh yeah, I really have to climb that."

Showing up at the gate with some money and absolutely no experience, he met another young man with a similar desire. They joined forces on the spot, found a guide and porters, and began climbing. By the time they reached the lip of the volcano several days later, and only a few hundred meters from the true summit, Vescovo was extremely sick. His body wasn't accustomed to the heights, he had a bad gastrointestinal bug, and the mountain had taken a punishing physical toll on his untrained body. He was forced to return to the bottom.

But in that first climb, he was bitten—hard—by the climbing bug. "I really liked the adventure part of it, of not knowing what was going to happen next, of would we make it around the next bend," he recalls. "I vowed I'd go home, train properly, work out very hard, and come back and reach the summit." A full decade later he did return, and climbed to the summit and back in just three days versus the normal six or seven.

While working at Bain & Company in San Francisco from 1987 to 1988, he was offered a PhD scholarship at the Massachusetts Institute of Technology (MIT) to study defense analysis. He matriculated at MIT but ended up pursuing and earning a master's degree in Political Science in just one year. His focus was on conventional military warfare analysis, statistics, and operations research. He wrote a master's thesis titled "The Balance of Air Power in Central Europe: A Quantitative and Qualitative Analysis"—a series of increasingly complex mathematical simulations of theater-level air warfare in central Europe that determined, based on an analysis of relative pilot training, doctrine, and the weapons each country had, who would have won an air war.

He attributes much of his academic success, as well as his later success in business, to his faith in math. He often says, "I may not have deep faith in a lot of things, like religion, but I do have deep faith in math." It's one of the maxims that guides his life, both in his investment ventures and in his exploration.

"There's a great line from the movie *Margin Call* where they are talking to a young analyst who has a PhD and he explains what his thesis was about," he related. "His boss says to him, 'So . . . you're a rocket scientist.' He says, 'I was.' They ask, 'Then why are you here on Wall Street?' The guy replied: 'It's all just numbers really, you're just changing what you're adding up.' "

From 1989 into 1990, Vescovo returned to Dallas and moved in with his father, who lived alone after his divorce years earlier. He took a humdrum job at a large telephone company to earn some money and recover from what had been a mentally exhausting experience at MIT. At the phone company, however, he came to understand the 9-to-5 mentality and the different priorities people had in their lives—like family above all—and usually doing only what was asked.

"I heard water cooler conversations about 'how can I make this new initiative go away,' 'how can we stretch out this work,' and 'this is the way we've always done things, so stop rocking the boat by trying to make it better,' " he recalls. "I learned how organizations are *really* resistant to change, though at the time I really didn't know how a direct experience of how people 'on the line' often thought would help me when I later worked to turn around such companies. People on the line just have very different priorities from management and owners. Success requires that you understand people and their priorities even if they are different from your own."

He moved into the world of high finance by taking a job at Lehman Brothers in New York in 1990 to 1991, during the *Liar's Poker* era. While working for Lehman, Vescovo was contacted by a Navy recruiter who told him about a special program for people proficient in foreign languages. He pursued the program, and following Condi Rice's advice, joined the U.S. Navy as a reserve intelligence officer and, in 1993, was commissioned as an ensign.

"I felt that joining the reserves was a way to participate in something bigger than myself," he says. "And I was absolutely fascinated with everything about the military."

Climbing fast became part of who he was, as well as his elixir in life. At age twenty-five, in 1991, he climbed Mount Elbrus in Russia. He went on a commercial expedition with nine people, but was one of only three that made it to the summit. While the group was on the mountain, there was a coup in Moscow, and they had to wait a few days before returning to Moscow. It was a tense time. "When we left Moscow, the hammer and sickle flag was flying, but when we came back, it was the Russian flag," he says. "The world literally changed while we were on the mountain."

In 1992, Vescovo was transferred to Saudi Arabia for a year, where he worked for the Saudi Ministry of Defense in the Economic Offset Projects Office analyzing business ventures proposed to them by foreign contractors. There, he learned Arabic and traveled throughout the Middle East. He returned to the U.S. to attend Harvard Business School, from 1992 to 1994, again living the life of "an intense nerd," as he sums it up, and focusing on high-order finance and learning how to value technology. He graduated in the top 5 percent of his class and was named a Baker Scholar.

His next climbing challenge came in 1993 when he attempted to summit Aconcagua in Argentina, the highest mountain in South America. A few hundred feet from the top, he fell and was badly injured. His team was ascending, unroped. Vescovo put his foot on a boulder, jarring it and causing a rockslide. He slid down the mountain with rocks bouncing around him and was knocked unconscious for a minute. When he came to, he couldn't speak and had excruciating lower back pain where a boulder had impacted his spine, and his right leg was partially paralyzed.

The group was too high for a helicopter rescue so a team of four French climbers and his own team helped him down to base camp. Suffering from hypothermia, he was stabilized and then medevacked to a hospital the following day. He ended up spending months in physical therapy and ultimately made a full recovery.

"Victor is always pushing himself to ultimate limits," his sister says. "Being close to death is something that brings life into focus for him. It's how he finds meaning."

His work life took a turn in 1994 when he returned to Bain & Company and formed the most important relationship of his business life, with Ted Beneski, the co-head of Bain's Dallas office. Beneski gave Vescovo the most complex deals. In a two-year period, Vescovo worked on the Continental Airlines turnaround, reliability process improvement at Dell Computer, and the merger integration of global aerospace giants Lockheed and Martin Marietta.

In his time away from work he focused on training and climbing. Two years after his fall on Aconcagua, he returned to Argentina and reached the summit of the mountain on his second attempt. A year later, he spent three weeks climbing Denali, also known as Mount McKinley, the highest peak in North America.

During this period, Vescovo was assigned to "Top Gun" on the Naval Reserve side. For four weeks a year on and off, he taught intelligence officers how to brief pilots on combat operations. He went on active duty for half a year in 1996, serving on the USS *Nimitz* in the Persian Gulf, and on the USS *Blue Ridge*. In 1999, he was mobilized for the Kosovo War in Bosnia, where he was directly involved in planning and assessing the effectiveness of NATO's bombing campaign against Serbia.

His military service was sent into high gear on September 11, 2001, in the wake of the terrorist attacks on U.S. soil. That night, Vescovo received a phone call that he was being mobilized again.

"Within the span of a week after 9/11, my girl-friend and I broke up, I left my job, sent my dog to live with my sister, moved out of my apartment and was on a plane to Pearl Harbor," he recalls. "I pretty much ended up in a vault and didn't come up for air for fifteen months."

He was made a Naval Intelligence officer, and was sent to the Joint Intelligence Center, Pacific, located at Pearl Harbor, to work on counter-terrorism analysis in the Pacific rim, primarily in the Philippines, Bangladesh, and Indonesia, based on his knowledge of Islamic culture and fluency in Arabic. This stint on active duty lasted fifteen months, and ended in December 2002. Over the course of the next five years, he would return to work in counterterrorism from time to time. During his time overseas, for fun, he wrote a book titled *The Atlas of World Statistics*, a fairly esoteric mashup of statistics and cartography. After his active duty stint ended, he climbed Mount Vinson in Antarctica, its highest peak.

It was when Victor was serving in Pearl Harbor that he received the most tragic news of his life: his sister, Valerie, had committed suicide. The middle child in the family, Valerie worked as an MD, licensed as an anesthesiologist in Portland, Oregon. It was known that she had battled with acute depression since her teenage years and was pushing through a rough period in her life, but like so many cases, it wasn't known just how serious hers was. Vescovo received emergency leave to attend the funeral. While he doesn't hide what happened, like most personal issues it's not a subject he is willing to spend much time delving into. The death of his sister, however, served as a continual reminder that life is short and that he must take every experience to its fullest point. Like many before him, Victor coped by turning his full attention to work.

His next business venture would become his most significant, one that drove his net worth well beyond $100 million and allowed him to buy a six-seat Embraer Phenom jet and a Eurocopter 120 helicopter, both of which he pilots. It came in 2002 when he started the Dallas-based private equity firm Insight Equity as a founding partner.

Formed by Ted Beneski, Ross Gatlin, and Vescovo, Insight Equity specializes in turn-arounds and business enhancement for mid-market industrial companies with revenues usually around $100 million. The firm has raised more than $1.4 billion in four capital raises and deployed it in a wide variety of industries, including heavy construction, energy, defense, industrial pollution control, and electronics. At the time Vescovo began contemplating diving the five oceans, he was serving as interim CEO of one company and chairman of four others.

"I guess I've become pretty good at time management, that, and I can type really fast, which helps," he says. "I'm not much for vacations either."

And there was climbing to be done. In 2008, he first attempted to summit Mount Everest but made it only halfway up. Battling frostbite on his fingers, he descended. "I also wasn't psychologically ready," he says. "My stepmom was undergoing chemotherapy and other things in my life were filling my head, and it just didn't feel right. You don't climb that mountain when you're distracted and it doesn't *feel* right."

He returned to Mount Everest in 2010. After a month and a half of climbing, on the final push to the summit, a clear weather forecast turned into a snowstorm. The guides and the Sherpa huddled together to make the call whether to go for the summit or return to the base. The weather window was closing and it was now or never for this climb. They had plenty of oxygen and the climbers were strong, so the decision was made to go. Victor's personal Sherpa on summit day was none other than Kami Rita Sherpa, who now holds the record for most summits of Everest in history, at twenty-four. That gave him no small degree of confidence, and the storm cleared almost all other climbers from the mountain, giving his team an all-important clear shot to the top.

On May 28, 2010, at 8:20 A.M., Victor reached the summit. Because of the poor weather and the threat of the storm worsening, his group spent all of fifteen minutes at the highest point on the planet. The hike down to the helicopter to take them off the mountain lasted three and a half days.

"In mountain climbing, it's not all about reaching the top, it's also about coming back down. It doesn't count if you don't come back," Vescovo often says.

The following year, he completed the "seven summits" by climbing Carstensz Pyramid in Irina Java, Indonesia, the highest mountain in Australia/Oceania. He then went on to ski the North and South Poles, making him the thirty-eighth person to complete the Explorers' Grand Slam.

He traces his philosophy of climbing and exploration to Roald Amundsen, the Norwegian explorer of the polar regions in the late 1800s and early 1900s, who was the type of explorer Vescovo admires and aspires to be. Amundsen was very methodical in his preparations and left as little as possible to chance. This was very much in contrast to Robert Falcon Scott, who led a separate expedition to the South Pole five weeks after Amundsen. Because of poor planning, Scott and his team that went with him all died.

"If the epitome of talent in war is to win without fighting, the height of skill in exploration is to achieve your objective with no heroics needed,"

Vescovo says. "Amundsen said—more or less—that adventure is a sign of bad planning. He *worked the problems* so that when he made the trek, he had the correct solutions to the problems. He did that through extensive preparation, realistic assumptions, thorough planning, and ruthless discipline in execution. Heroism is exciting to read about—planning and preparation aren't. But when you are actually the one doing the exploring, believe me, you want a no-drama expedition."

Owing partly to the danger of climbing, his side career in the Navy, and an almost obsessive dedication to his work, Vescovo has never married and has no children. He also points out that his family's matrimonial track record is poor. His mother was married four times and thrice-divorced, his father had two marriages and one divorce, his older sister the same, and his younger sister one divorce. Even all of his uncles, aunts, and cousins are divorced without exception. Adding to this, his best friend from high school has married four times. Vescovo figured his odds were not good.

In 2010, Vescovo met Monika Allajbeu. A native of Albania, the statuesque Allajbeu has the features of a model with the warmth of personality of a girl who grew up in a large family. She often calls Vescovo "Lance," his middle name used during his childhood. A year after they began dating, she moved into Vescovo's house in north Dallas, and made plans to enter dental school. She prides herself on giving Vescovo space to do what he wants.

Never marrying has also allowed Vescovo not to feel responsible to anyone, such as children or a wife, should something go horribly wrong during his extreme adventures. As he points out, he has nearly died on a mountain twice. He also adds: "There's too much to do to be tied down. And, maybe, I think I would lose that edge that pushes you to your limit."

Part of Vescovo's drive to explore dangerous pursuits may be explained by what Dr. Glenn Singleman, an MD, refers to as the Exploration Gene Theory, which helps explain why certain people need to seek out thrilling pursuits to feel fully alive. Singleman, who holds a world record in base-jumping, has studied this phenomenon and served on several exploration expeditions.

The theory is rooted in research done by Dr. Marvin Zuckerman of the University of Delaware. He found that on the DRD4 gene on chromosome 11, people have a different number of copies, between two and eleven. The gene itself codes for dopamine receptors in the central nervous system and measures their sensitivity.

"If a person has two copies of the DRD4 gene, they have sensitive dopamine receptors in their central nervous system," Singleman explains. "The importance of that is that dopamine is the 'feel good' neurotransmitter of the central nervous system. Every time that person feels a WOW moment, that is dopamine in action, the feel of being really invigorated. So if you have sensitive dopamine receptors, you don't need much stimulation to get your dopamine receptors activated. That's if you have two copies. If you have eleven copies of the DRD4 gene, you have insensitive dopamine receptors in the central nervous system. That means to get that buzz, you have to have high sensations."

Singleman says these sensation-seekers tend to be the race car drivers, test pilots, skydivers, and mountain climbers. They are also people with a greater propensity for other dangers, including criminal behavior.

"The brains of these people are wired different," Singleman says. "People like Victor have to undertake these extreme adventures to get that dopamine release. They also respond differently to trouble and are able to overcome a fear response when faced with extreme danger. Rather than being overwhelmed, they are able to reorient themselves, respond, and solve problems in life-threatening situations."

Singleman takes things a step further, saying that people like Vescovo are necessary to push the boundaries of what is possible. "To get into the possibility of the human condition, you have to have those 'test pilots,' like astronauts, who go out and test the boundaries," Singleman says. "They are essential to the health of society because otherwise we would be stuck in place on so many levels."

Contemplating the existential question of "why attempt to dive the five oceans?" Vescovo acknowledges the need within himself to undertake extreme adventures. "There's a certain group of people, genetically or otherwise, where it's a compulsion to attempt difficult things," he says. "Something inside drives us, whether it's psychosis or the exploration gene. To *not* do these things is *very* difficult for us because you feel you are not properly living within the constructs of your own personality. We feel like the horse in the cage before the race—raging against the steel constraints confining us.

"Building on that theme," he continues, "this adventure has the added enhancement to do something completely new, a lure all of its own. Is there a bit of egotism involved? Absolutely. But that's not the driving force."

So when Vescovo was completing the seven summits, he was trying to stave off a letdown by thinking about the nature of exploration, which had come into focus in the news as private missions to space were being planned by billionaires Sir Richard Branson, Elon Musk, and

Jeff Bezos. He needed a new challenge, a unique challenge that no one had achieved. The media was again talking about space, but what about the depths? Who had gone to the deepest points on the planet, to the bottom of the five oceans?

When he learned that no one had, it was time, Vescovo thought, for someone to try. For him, this pursuit would combine the thrill of climbing with the lessons he had learned in business, as it also presented major technological and organizational challenges. This would also call on skills from his naval background, both in terms of exploring the seas and the type of military-style planning that would be required. What started as a matter of curiosity fast became a goal, and he decided that he was at least going to find out if he had the wherewithal to finance such an undertaking, and if there were people who could help him get it done.

"I also found it objectionable that here we were in the year 2014—2014!—and we still have not been to the bottom of all five of our oceans," he says. "In some respects, it comes down to that. Someone should have done this. I have the resources to try, and it sounds like a fun adventure. So I started looking seriously into just what would it take to accomplish that goal."

Sitting across from Vescovo at dinner that night in Dallas, his sister Victoria was convinced that he would somehow make this dream a reality.

"When Victor sets a goal and gets that look in his eyes, you know that is going to happen," his sister says.

It's no understatement saying that she held the minority belief for quite some time.

CHAPTER 2
THE SEARCH FOR A SUB

If curiosity is the driver of all exploration, it has been in limited supply when it comes to deep ocean diving and the vessels necessary to reach extreme depths. The deep diving submersible world was a fairly small community with a limited track record, as Victor Vescovo discovered in 2014 when he began researching how he could reach the bottom of the five oceans, and who had attempted—and succeeded—in reaching the ocean floor in the past.

The first vessel to reach the bottom of what was believed to be the deepest point of the oceans was a bathyscaphe (meaning "deep ship") named the *Trieste* after the Italian city where it was built. Piloted by U.S. Navy lieutenant Don Walsh and Swiss engineer Jacques Piccard, the son of the bathyscaphe's designer, the *Trieste* reached the bottom of the Challenger Deep in 1960. The Challenger Deep is a long gash in the Mariana Trench in the Pacific Ocean, off the coast of Guam. The *Trieste*'s depthometer measured water pressure and plotted it on a paper cylinder. It recorded—after some technical corrections—a final revised depth of 10,912 meters (35,800 feet).

The *Trieste* was a fairly basic craft that worked much like a hot-air balloon—only it did so underwater. (Though often called submarines, bathyscaphes are not technically submarines because they are built like hot-air balloons and have limited mobility. A submarine is a self-contained submerging vessel in which the crew can live for prolonged periods of time. This is in contrast to a submersible, which cannot be deployed as an independent vehicle, and requires a surface support ship.) In fact, the *Trieste* was designed by the Swiss scientist Auguste Piccard, who was known for his record-breaking helium balloon flights before turning his attention to bathyscaphes. Piccard applied the principles of ballooning to the design of his deep-sea craft.

The *Trieste*, which weighed some 150 tons, was composed of a steel sphere large enough for two aquanauts and had a single acrylic window from which the pilots could view their surroundings. The average hull thickness of the sphere was seven inches, the same as its Plexiglas viewport. On top of the sphere were several tanks holding 34,200 gallons of aviation fuel. The concept was that the gasoline in the tanks was lighter than water and can't be compressed, thereby providing buoyancy to the heavy craft. To send the bathyscaphe down the water column, large air tanks on its top were filled with water to initiate descent. Two large tubs on the bottom each contained eight tons of steel shots that would be released at the ocean's floor for the craft to regain buoyancy and ascend.

On the *Trieste*'s Challenger Deep dive, while passing through 9,000 meters, a secondary window that was in the entrance tube to the sphere, but was not a pressure boundary, cracked. Walsh and Piccard looked at each other in a moment of severe anxiety. But when they realized they weren't dead, they shared a nervous laugh and continued their descent. The extreme pressure had compressed the cracked acrylic and sealed it from leaking.

In its first and only dive in the Challenger Deep, the *Trieste* took 4 hours and 48 minutes to reach the bottom, stayed just 20 minutes because its landing impaired visibility, and then took 3 hours and 15 minutes to return to the surface.

Part of the reason it went down only that one time was that the Navy found out that after one of the *Trieste*'s test dives, the sphere had shifted slightly, and epoxy glue was applied before the Challenger Deep dive. When Walsh later sat down with a Navy admiral about future dives, he lectured Walsh, "In the Navy, we don't glue the hull of a sub." Walsh also says that Piccard told the brass at Office of Naval Research, who were funding the program, that he did not think the sphere was safe for full ocean depth dives.

The *Trieste*, however, was refitted several times and used in many subsequent government underwater missions. It was retired in 1964, and in 1980 was placed in the U.S. Navy Museum in Washington, D.C.

The French Navy built the next major deep-diving submersible in 1961, the *Archimède*, their second bathyscaphe. Like the *Trieste*, it too used gasoline for buoyancy. In this case, the gasoline used was 42,000 gallons of hexane, the lightest gasoline available.

One main difference between the *Trieste* and the *Archimède* was in the sphere that housed the pilots. The *Trieste* had three pieces of steel forged together—and glued together, as mentioned—while the *Archimède* pilot capsule was one welded piece of steel. The result was that the *Archimède* was far stronger. The Trieste had a safety factor of 1.1 at full ocean depth, but the added ability to withstand pressure gave the *Archimède* a factor of 3.

In its history, the *Archimède* made multiple deep ocean dives. In 1962, it reached a depth of 9,560 meters (31,350 feet) across multiple dives in the northwestern Pacific Ocean. Then, in 1964, the *Archimède* dived to what was believed to be the deepest point in the Atlantic Ocean in the Puerto Rico Trench, though the location turned out to be incorrect. There was never a mandate to dive and explore the deepest points of the other oceans—these were exclusively scientific, not record-breaking, missions.

More advanced manned submersibles were built in the ensuing years, but progress was slow, at best. The years of intermittent deep-diving activity in the late 1950s began to temper as media, public, and government attention drifted to the "space race."

The *Alvin*, a two-pilot, one-passenger sub, was built in 1964 by the U.S. Office of Naval Research and operated by the Woods Hole Oceanographic Institution (WHOI). The cost was pegged at $1 million. The 23-foot, 17-ton sub, which had two robotic arms, made headlines for taking Robert Ballard to the *Titanic* wreck in 1986 and for exploring the Deepwater Horizon oil spill. The sub has made more than 4,400 dives conducting research, diving to depths of 4,500 meters, and is still in use today.

The advantage of the *Alvin* over its predecessors was that it was far lighter. The lightness was created by using syntactic foam for buoyancy rather than the gasoline tanks used in the *Trieste* and the *Archimède*. Syntactic foam is composed of millions of hollow glass microspheres wrapped in an epoxy resin, and it is strong enough to withstand the pressure at deep depths while remaining buoyant.

"We would have eagerly adopted foam and

titanium if they were available to us," Walsh says. "The bathyscaphes and their huge quantities of highly flammable hydrocarbons were essentially large bombs, a constant source of concern to all of us. But that's all we had."

Four *Alvin*-class submersibles were subsequently built, and they were continuously upgraded since their original launch, with depth capability increasing and productivity enhanced with evolving modern systems. Still, none was even remotely capable of diving to the oceans' deepest points.

In 1984, the French built a follow-up to the *Archimède* named the *Nautile*, operated by a new French government ocean agency. Also called the SM-97, meaning it was capable of surveying 97 percent of the planet's ocean waters, the *Nautile* could dive to 6,000 meters.

The interior diameter of the *Nautile* was the same as the *Archimède*'s, but its sphere was constructed of titanium, making it far lighter, and therefore easier to launch and recover. It was used to dive to the *Titanic* wreck multiple times and also to search for the black boxes from the downed Air France flight 447, an Airbus 380 that crashed into the Atlantic Ocean on June 1, 2009.

The *Mir*, a three-person submersible, came next in 1987. It was similar to the *Nautile* in many regards. Capable of reaching 6,000 meters, the *Mir 1* and its updated version, the *Mir 2*, were also used several times to dive the *Titanic* wreck, at 3,800 meters, which fast become a benchmark of respectability in the deep submersible vehicle community. The ship that carried the submersible, the *Akademik Mstislav Keldysh* (or *"Keldish"* for short in Western nomenclature), had a more sophisticated launch and recovery system than the *Alvin*, allowing it to dive in rougher seas. However, the *Mir*'s drawback was that anyone using it for expeditions had to supply their own cameras and other science-related equipment.

The technological bar in deep ocean submersibles was advanced by the Japanese government with the development of *Shinkai*, a three-person submersible put into service in 1989 that could dive to 6,500 meters. It was owned and run by the Japan Agency for Marine-Earth Science and Technology, which received funding from a consortium of large companies. Consequently, in its time, the *Shinkai* was outfitted with the most advanced electronics, the highest resolution cameras, the most accurate sonar, and high capacity batteries that allowed for longer dives. Its support ship, the *Yokosuka*, also had a multibeam sonar to measure the diving depths.

In 2010, the Chinese government built the deepest diving submersible since the *Trieste*, the *Jialong*, which reached a maximum depth of 7,062 meters (23,169 feet) in the Mariana

Trench in 2012. Two years later, when Vescovo was doing his research, it seemed to still be operational, though no one was sure of its true depth capabilities or what it was doing.

The common factor in almost all submersibles built and operated after 1964—until 2012—was that they were limited to diving in the top two thirds of the ocean. But they could not explore the absolute deeps.

The top 200 meters of the oceans is known as the Epipelagic Zone, where common sea life exists. From 200 to 1,000 meters is the Twilight Zone, which is just beyond the reach of sunlight and home to bioluminescent species. The Midnight Zone stretches from 1,000 to 4,000 meters and favors sea creatures with slow metabolic rates. This is followed by the Abyssal Zone, from 4,000 meters to 6,000 meters, an area so deep that it is unaffected by surface weather. The Hadal Zone starts at 6,000 meters and goes down to the bottom of the ocean at more than 10,900 meters, and this is where it becomes difficult for life.

The name "Hadal" is derived from the Greek god of the underworld, Hades, as the ocean depths are often regarded as dark and scary as hell itself. The deepest parts of the Hadal Zone exist in the large ocean trenches that are knife-like canyons in the seafloor. These were formed by tectonic activity as the seafloor crustal plates converge, at what are called convergence zones, with one pushing under the other, a process called subduction. This occurs at continental boundaries when the more dense seafloor plate pushes under a relatively buoyant continental plate. The frictional forces result in significant terrestrial volcanic activity. Exploration of the Hadal Zone in manned submersibles has been virtually nonexistent, as scientists have relied on remotely operated vehicles, or ROVs.

Until 2012, of all the active submersibles, only *Jialong* could reliably dive into the Hadal Zone— and it appeared to do that rarely. That year, the bar was raised when a submersible capable of reaching full ocean depth was constructed.

Named the *Deepsea Challenger*, the submersible was designed by Australian Ron Allum for an expedition led by filmmaker James Cameron and financed by National Geographic, Rolex, and other partners. Though the sub was tested in a pressure chamber at Penn State University before diving, it was a prototype and was not certified by any international organization or depth-rated for commercial use. Its cost, according to published reports and those on Cameron's mission team, was in the $10- to $12-million range, not including several million dollars spent on the expedition.

The "Kawasaki racing-green" submersible was

built for practicality, and not aesthetics. It was 24 feet long and only 43 inches wide, so small inside that the pilot had to squeeze his body into the sphere and lie flat rather than sit up. The space was so constrained that he could not fully extend his arms.

The sub's steel capsule was 2.5 inches thick and weighed 11.8 tons. It had twelve exterior thrusters that allowed the pilot, using joysticks, to "drive" the sub just above the seafloor. The two keys to the sub's full ocean depth capability were its syntactic foam created by Allum and called Isofloat, which was used for buoyancy, and powerful lithium batteries with rapid recharging systems. The sub was outfitted with 3D cameras and had a mechanical arm for picking up sediment and rock samples that could be deposited into a retractable compartment on the sub.

After four test dives in Sydney Harbor and off the coast of New Britain in the Pacific, Cameron went for the bottom of the Challenger Deep. On March 26, 2012, Cameron successfully piloted the submersible to the bottom of the eastern portion of the Challenger Deep, making it only the second mission to reach the nadir, and the first solo mission.

Weather and time constraints forced Cameron to dive at night. He spent two and a half hours exploring the bottom. When he returned to the surface, the support ship had difficulty locating him. The ship called on billionaire Paul Allen's yacht, which was nearby, to help guide it to Cameron's position and recover him.

During the dive, the sub encountered a series of problems, many of which were caused by an accelerated schedule that resulted in the use of what turned out to be some subpar parts. Many of the Chinese-made thrusters reportedly failed, and there were multiple system failures, though none life-threatening. Though plans were made to repair it, the submersible never dived again.

Vescovo was surprised by his research. In all, there were only five working submersibles capable of going below 7,500 meters. All five were owned and operated by governments. Since the *Mirs* went out of service in dives below a few hundred meters in 2005, there wasn't any submersible that could reach the *Titanic*, at about 3,900 meters. Only two missions, fifty-two years apart, had reached the bottom of the Challenger Deep in the Pacific Ocean, and *no one* had reached the bottom of the other four oceans. Moreover, no one had really tried. How was that even possible, he asked himself.

More research revealed that scientists didn't even definitively *know* where the deepest points of the Atlantic, Arctic, Indian, and Southern Oceans were because they hadn't been properly mapped with modern technology. The bathymetric maps of the oceans that existed were inconsistent. Early bathymetric study of the oceans, which involved lowering cables to measure the depth, were wildly inaccurate. Updated methods of using an echosounder, or sonar, to ping a beam of sound to the seafloor were more reliable, but a lack of interest or funding had led to incomplete data across vast stretches of all five oceans.

Why had no government gone to the bottom of the oceans? Certainly, the U.S. government wouldn't likely fund such a mission, and even if they did, it would take years, be mired in red tape and appropriations and cost far more than it needed, he reasoned. "What is an elephant?" he liked to joke to people. "It's a mouse built to government specifications."

He kept digging. Had any private investor tried?

Sort of, was the answer.

Sir Richard Branson, the billionaire owner of Virgin Atlantic, announced a mission to dive the five oceans, but that had turned out to be more sizzle than substance. Virgin Oceanic's *DeepFlight Challenger* submarine was unveiled in April 2011, with Branson describing its mission to dive to the bottom of all five oceans as "the last great challenge for humans," something Vescovo agreed with.

The *DeepFlight Challenger* was designed in 2000 by Graham Hawkes, a well-known British sub builder, for the adventurer Steve Fossett to make the first solo dive to the bottom of the Challenger Deep. But when Fossett died in a plane crash in 2007, the project was put on hold. It was subsequently purchased by investor Chris Welsh, who then partnered with Branson.

Designed to look like an airplane with a large front window, the single-pilot sub was about 24 feet long and had a 10-foot wingspan. Initial pressure testing showed that the sub would likely only be able to do a single full ocean depth dive, but even that proved to be optimistic. The vessel's domed viewport showed signs of cracking during testing. The pressure hull, made of carbon fiber, also would not be able to withstand sustained pressure on repeat dives to full ocean depth.

Though the company's website promised "five dives, five oceans, two years, one epic adventure," the sub made only five shallow test dives, during which it encountered a series of insurmountable problems. In 2014, Branson put the entire project on ice, but didn't rule out returning to it. "Starting a new venture takes a 'screw it, let's do it' attitude and finding the right partners to help us achieve the unthinkable," he said at the time. "However, business is also about knowing when to change tack. We are still highly passionate about exploring the bottom of the ocean. However, we are now widening the focus of the project and looking for new technology to help us explore the ocean and democratize access at reduced cost and increased safety."

Since then, there have been incomplete reports of an ostensibly private Chinese venture, called the "Rainbow Fish Project," to build a full ocean depth submersible and custom support ship. But the best information indicated that the project was millions of dollars over budget and its completion date kept being pushed back. And besides, Vescovo wasn't sure the Chinese would be excited about loaning their craft to a former U.S. Naval Intelligence officer.

It was time, Vescovo thought instead, to build his very own reliable submersible to send him where no one had gone before.

The first option for a submersible was to purchase the *Deepsea Challenger*. "Logically, I thought that if that sub still exists and given that it had gone to the bottom of the Challenger Deep, then it could go to the bottom of all the oceans," he says.

Vescovo also reasoned that it would be less expensive to buy an existing sub and update it than to have one built. He found that after its success diving the Challenger Deep, the *Deepsea Challenger* had been donated to the Woods Hole Oceanographic Institution on Cape Cod.

In the spring of 2014, Vescovo contacted WHOI, and explained that he was interested in purchasing the *Deepsea Challenger*. As it wasn't a normal inquiry, and perhaps not entirely believable, a few months passed before he received a response. That July, the WHOI special projects manager, David Gallo, invited Vescovo to see the sub.

Vescovo flew to Boston, rented a car and drove to Cape Cod. The two met at a coffee shop to discuss Vescovo's intentions, and then headed over to see the *Deepsea Challenger*. Vescovo was very surprised at what he saw.

The history-making sub was crammed into a corner in the back of a large warehouse, sort of a metaphor for where deep ocean diving had gone since Cameron's mission. It looked worn out. There were cables hanging out of the hull, and several of the thrusters appeared to be barely attached. Gallo explained that the batteries and the thrusters would need to be completely replaced, along with a very long litany of other items.

"It was almost like he was discouraging me from taking it over," Vescovo recalls. "He kept calling it a prototype and saying it needed a full-on rebuild. What I was also surprised to see was just how small the interior was in real life. It was basically a small bubble that the pilot has to be shoehorned into."

Vescovo left Woods Hole wondering what a refit would cost even if he chose to pursue it, and shifting his thinking toward having a sub built from scratch. Still, he followed up with Woods Hole a few more times, but he never heard back.

The fate of the *Deepsea Challenger* would later take a bizarre turn. In July 2015, the sub was loaded onto a flatbed truck en route to a container ship that would transport it to Australia for an exhibition. Driving on Interstate 95 near Stonington, Connecticut, the transport truck's brakes malfunctioned and ignited the rear wheels, catching the sub on fire. A part of the sub's bright green hull was charred. Later, the sub was relocated to California for refurbishment with reports that it was eventually headed for a maritime museum in Australia.

As it became apparent that the *Deepsea Challenger* would not be the best option, or even a viable one, Vescovo turned his attention to finding a company that could build a full ocean depth submersible. He happened upon the website for Triton Submarines, a small company in Vero Beach, Florida, that appeared to be a well-regarded submersible manufacturer. His interest was sparked by Triton's affiliation with Ron Allum, the designer of the *Deepsea Challenger*.

He was particularly encouraged that the

company's website actually advertised a full ocean depth submersible, called a "36,000/3"— meaning a submersible that could dive to 36,000 feet with 3 people inside—though there was little information about it. That was exactly what was needed.

On September 14, 2014, Vescovo emailed Triton Submarines' head of marketing and sales, Mark Deppe. He expressed interest in leasing a Triton 36,000/3 if Triton had one available.

"To be quite direct, my intention is to partner with a firm and support team to journey not just to the Challenger Deep, but the other deepest points of the world's four other oceans," he wrote. "This has never been done, and I would very much like to expend the resources and time to be the first to do so."

He also mentioned that the dream to dive the ocean was an extension of his recently completed quest to climb the seven summits. And he indicated that he was the cofounder of a successful private equity firm and had the financial resources to see such a deep ocean diving project through.

A response quickly came back, and a call was set up. It turned out, however, Triton had a *vision* for a full ocean depth sub, but they hadn't actually *built* one. No client had stepped up and ordered it, so all that existed was a colorful drawing and a dream of what might be possible.

And no one was quite sure how much it would cost. Undeterred, Vescovo decided he would meet the Triton team and find out just what the possibilities were.

CHAPTER 3
THE SUB BUILDERS

At the time Victor Vescovo contacted Triton Submarines in 2014, the company was housed in a nondescript, warehouse-style building off the beaten path, down the street from a Burger King in Vero Beach. The manufacturing floor resembled a marine version of the Wright Brothers' bicycle shop, with spare parts strewn out over workbenches and the floor littered with circuit boards, propellers, and widgets all shapes and sizes for the subs in progress. The communal offices were in a two-story attachment to the warehouse. The thin, wood-paneled walls caused employees to joke about having to wear headphones for privacy. Behind the main building was a cement courtyard used for assembly space, and at the rear of a property was a second manufacturing building.

The company was formed in 2007 by L. Bruce Jones and Patrick Lahey. Jones and Lahey met when Jones was running U.S. Submarines, which he did from 1987 through 2007. Lahey worked for Jones on several projects and then the two decided to form a company to concentrate on building small submersibles.

"I gave Patrick half the business with the understanding that I would not be there full-time and that he would run the day-to-day operations," Jones explains. Though Triton was headquartered in Florida, Jones continued to reside in rural Idaho. So Lahey became the operational leader of the company, Jones its marketer.

The two men are Type A personalities and share many things in common, but have very different styles in business.

Jones, 63, is a bear of a man with a round face that suits his jolly demeanor. He punctuates his stories, good and bad, with a hearty chuckle. He's not shy about expressing his role in the company's projects. Though this has led to his reputation as a self-promoter, he characterizes it as being an advocate for Triton. He often takes a very direct approach that can rub clients the wrong way, something he says can be necessary to protect his team and keep things moving forward.

Lahey, seven years his junior, has spiked white hair and tanned skin from spending much of the last thirty-six years on ship decks deploying subs. He casually drops f-bombs, using them positively, negatively, and angrily in equal doses. Appearing a bit high-strung to some, he carries the weight of the company's projects on his shoulders, literally walking with them pitched forward, but he shines a beacon of optimism on every situation. He takes a back seat to the client and operates under the premise that the client is always right—or if the client isn't, he's at least very deferential to their view.

Both men came to love the ocean at an early age. Jones grew up all over the world in mostly port cities, living in Hong Kong, Manila, Singapore, and Jakarta, as well as on oil rigs for periods of time. In total, he has visited 121 countries and lived in 20. His mother was a civil engineer, his father a marine engineer. His grandfather also made his living in the maritime industry, owning a large marine fleet construction company and, according to Jones, had a role in inventing containerized shipping.

Jones learned to scuba dive at age eight in the Persian Gulf, triggering an immediate fascination for underwater exploration. When he was in the eighth grade and living in Singapore, his parents were displeased with the school choices so they sent him to boarding school in the U.S. at Culver Military Academy in northern Indiana. "I hated it, but I appreciated what it did for me," he says. "And I learned to fly airplanes there."

He later attended Trinity University and after graduating went to work in gemology. The interest continues to this day, as he keeps what he calls the world's most advanced private gemological lab on the second floor of his Idaho home.

After his first marriage ended in divorce, Jones met his current wife of thirty-two years, Liz. The two shared the same adventuresome spirit. When they met, Liz had just finished sailing around the world. They now regularly go on trips in their small plane, ride in their hot-air balloon, and take excursions in their motor home.

Jones is a *bon vivant* who will sip champagne in the afternoon if the mood suits him. He is full of colorful stories, many of which sound slightly exaggerated or even apocryphal. To wit: "When we were treasure hunting in the Philippines, I made a recovery of $300 million of gold bullion, but [President Ferdinand] Marcos was my partner and he took it all, and we got escorted to the airport at gunpoint."

Lahey's love affair with the oceans also started in his childhood. He spent his early years in landlocked Ottawa, Canada, but when he was seven, his father moved the family to Barbados for three years. Lahey's new backyard was the crystalline waters of the Atlantic Ocean.

"The ocean made an indelible impression on me," Lahey recalls. "Looking at it every day solidified my desire to have a life of the ocean. There's a great line from Jacques Cousteau: 'The sea, once it casts its spell, holds one in its net of wonder forever.' I'm one who found himself under that spell."

Lahey got into the sub game in his late teens.

He had become a certified scuba diver at thirteen, and by the time he turned eighteen, he was working as a commercial diver in the oil and gas industry.

At that time, the industry used manned submersibles for exploration. The submersibles were more like oversized, wearable diving suits. The pilot slid inside a pressure-controlled tube that barely had enough room for him to move his arms to operate the controls.

Lahey made his first solo dive in one of those subs at age twenty-one off the coast of Santa Barbara, California, to inspect an oil rig at 1,400 feet. "I vividly remember the cobalt blue water all around me and the sense of liberation I had," he says. "As a diver, I was accustomed to spending time in a decompression chamber when I came up. In a sub, you don't have to do that. I decided at the moment I surfaced that subs would be the focus of my professional life."

Triton started small and experienced growing pains in a very niche business. The first two Triton submersibles, which were built when Jones and Lahey were still at U.S. Submarines, were 1,000/2s, meaning two people could occupy the capsule and dive to a maximum depth of 1,000 feet. The company then graduated to building acrylic-sphered 3,300/3s that look like aquatic spaceships. These became the company's bread and butter.

Triton's first three years were "dismal with small growth," as Jones characterizes them. The company was manufacturing one to two subs a year. It had persistent issues with suppliers, such as when the UK company that built the acrylic spheres for its 3,300/3s delivered ones that were yellowish and of dubious durability. The company actually managed to destroy two spheres. Triton switched to a German manufacturer, but there was a long research and development cycle that slowed Triton's output before the company arrived at a new method to make optically clear and stronger acrylic spheres.

By 2011, the pace increased and Triton's staff had grown from the original three full-timers to thirty-six. Revenues were also growing, at a rate of 25 percent per year. High net worth clients began ordering Triton subs, such as billionaire investor Ray Dalio, who owns two. By 2014, when Vescovo contacted Triton about building a full ocean depth submersible, the company had increased its output to two or three subs a year and had made twelve.

"Triton has always been a little bit of a Skunk Works," Lahey says, referring to Lockheed Martin's legendary development shop that coined the term for innovative undertakings that operate outside research norms. "It's an unusual place full of eccentric people, but people who are passionate about what they do and who infuse their energy into every part they make."

When Jones first read Vescovo's query, he wasn't sure what to make of a Texan who said he wanted to fund a deep diving sub. Jones knew everyone in the sub world, but he had never heard of Vescovo. "Patrick and I live on a steady diet of rejection," he says. "We've been through it all. Every wacko that wants a submarine over the last thirty years, we've heard from them. But Victor was a very credible guy from the beginning and pretty easy to deal with."

Out of left field, as the two sides were just beginning a correspondence about the sub, Jones pitched Vescovo on a marijuana business investment for cannabis oil production in California and Washington. "My response was, 'Um . . . okay . . . no thanks," Vescovo says. "A bit of a yellow flag, too."

Based on Vescovo's strong interest in pursuing the full ocean depth sub, Triton began internally gathering information on what it would take to build it. The company was focused on its dream to build a sub with a transparent pressure boundary, essentially a glass sphere. The properties of glass are such that a perfect sphere could sustain the pressure, but there were a variety of drawbacks that came to light.

While the right type of high-pressure glass could bear the compressional stress, there could not be any type of glass-to-metallic interface. This meant the glass sphere would have to be a clamshell design with all the equipment necessary to power and operate the sub located inside the sphere. A further problem was that the glass company Triton had approached was proving unreliable.

Vescovo wasn't sold on the idea of a glass sphere for three passengers. "I went back to them and said, no, let's go tried and true," he says. "I don't want to sink a ton of money in bleeding-edge tech that may or may not work."

Triton was forced to abandon the idea and focus on something more practical. "There were obvious advantages to glass, but as Victor so eloquently put it, he wasn't interested in funding a science experiment," Lahey says. "And fair enough. It was a shrewd and fairly wise decision on his part because at the end of the day, as exciting as a glass pressure boundary is at full ocean depth, it's still far off and unknown."

During this time, on May 20, 2015, Triton invited Vescovo to the Bahamas to dive in one of their three-person submersibles, a Triton 3,300/3 (meaning a maximum depth of 3,300 feet with three passengers). Lahey had two Emirati clients on the ship. The two men were chatting away in Arabic when Victor walked in—and started talking to them in Arabic. Lahey was floored.

Vescovo had never been inside a sub, and the experience cemented his interest in pursuing a full ocean depth sub.

In the Bahamas, Vescovo also met the company's lead sub designer, John Ramsay, who was based in the UK. Ramsay, who is in his late thirties, has a boyish spirit about him, tousled hair, a thin scruff of facial hair, and eyes that open extra wide when he emphasizes a point.

Ramsay had started at Triton as a consultant in 2006 and went full time in 2012 after designing sixteen subs for Triton. Previously, he had worked in the UK building military-oriented submarine rescue systems, in which a small sub with a decompression chamber attached to it would dive to a larger submarine to bring people safely back to the surface.

Ramsay would be tasked with coming up with a workable design for the full ocean depth submersible. As complex as the undertaking would be, Ramsay operates on a fairly straight-forward philosophy of "if you can't explain it, you don't understand it."

"One of the objectives of that dive in the Bahamas was to prove to Victor the importance of being able to see out of the submarine with your own eyes and not just through cameras," Ramsay says. "At the time he wasn't interested in all the specialized requirements of a submersible, but we wanted him to see them."

Vescovo was immediately impressed with Ramsay. "He struck me as a child prodigy who grew up and got to build things he had only dreamed of," Vescovo says.

After the Bahamas dive, the discussions became more specific. Some basic questions had to be answered before Ramsay could begin the actual design. First among them was how many passengers the sub would carry.

Vescovo wanted to dive solo to the bottom of the deeps, and he wasn't convinced that having viewports was worth the expense or the risk. No full ocean depth submarine had ever had more than one viewport, and Triton wanted to put in *three*. Instead, he suggested they put several high-definition cameras on the outside to film the depths and show the pilot what was outside— referring to them as "virtual windows." He reasoned that a single-pilot sub would also be far roomier. What he was looking for was an elevator to the bottom of the ocean and back to the surface. "Let's just start from just the basics: put me in a metal ball, and drop me to the bottom," he only half-joked to Jones.

Both Jones and Lahey pushed back. They argued that a two-person sub with viewports had far more utility and ongoing value after Vescovo finished his expedition. "If you can't see out of the sub, what's the point?" Lahey said. If the sub held two people, the pilot and a passenger (such as a scientist or a filmmaker), they could dive and interact together. Finding a buyer for a two-person submersible with viewports would also be easier than selling a one-seater that you couldn't directly see out of. Triton also wanted to put a mechanical arm on the sub to collect sediment and rock samples.

"I talked to Patrick and I said, 'Victor, respectfully we are not going to build a one-person sub with no viewports,'" Jones says. "I told him, 'One, you will never be able to sell it, and two, you are not going to be able to do any science. You have the risk of this being perceived by the world as just doing an ego-motivated record attempt with a submarine that will have no future value.'"

As Jones pointed out to Vescovo, for different reasons, that was what had happened with the two previous deepest diving subs. Both the two-person *Trieste* and one-seater *Deepsea Challenger* only completed one dive to the Challenger Deep. While both were intended for multiple repeat dives to the Challenger Deep, neither sub attempted a second dive to full ocean depth, and the *Deepsea Challenger* ended up never diving again and was donated to a museum rather than sold.

"We convinced him to build a sub that would move the needle," Jones says. "We wanted to build a sub, not just for Victor, but for others to follow in his footsteps and continue ocean exploration. We wanted a sub that was fully accredited by an independent, third party agency that would attest to its capabilities."

There were only a handful of companies that certified submarines, and none had ever even been asked to certify one to full ocean depth. James Cameron and his team had pressure-tested the *Deepsea Challenger*, but it had not gone through an independent certification process, thereby leaving it classified as an experimental prototype.

The cost to have the sub certified would be in the range of $500,000, not including the pressurized testing of all components, which could be twice that much. Nevertheless, Jones and Lahey were pushing, insisting almost, that the sub they built for Vescovo be certified, primarily to add value for a potential buyer. "Certification of a full ocean depth submersible was a groundbreaking issue," Jones says. "Triton had never built a sub that had not been certified. Besides, many science organizations and other private individuals would never get in a sub if it is not certified."

Involving the certification company in the design phase was paramount, as the company would need to weigh in on decisions as they were made. Lahey had in mind using Det Norske Veritas-Germanischer Lloyd (DNV-GL), a German-Norwegian company that is the world's largest maritime classification society. The head of its submersible unit, Jonathan Struwe, thirty-four, was one of the most knowledgeable people in the world on submersibles, making him the ideal sounding board as the company built the sub.

"DNV-GL was far more receptive to the ideas being promoted for this new vehicle which was breaking from traditional configurations," Lahey said. "Jonathan became a co-designer from day one. He worked hand in glove with John Ramsay and added many of the clever design ideas."

Vescovo was eventually persuaded that a certified, two-person sub was the best idea. "It was clear that having a commercial vehicle that could execute tens of thousands of cycles to many depths over many decades was the way to go, and certification is what makes that possible," he said.

By June, the focus of the material for the hull had shifted from glass to metals. "That is a pretty fundamental decision: what are you going to make your house out of, brick or wood," Lahey says. "What to make the hull out of was the most significant initial decision that had to be made."

The issues with the hull were its physical diameter, the cost of material, and the corrosion properties. Furthermore, the diameter mattered because the hull could not be wider than the largest pressure-testing chamber in the world at the Krylov Shipbuilding Research Institute in Russia, or an entirely new facility would have to be built at an enormous cost.

Another variable was weight versus buoyancy. Regardless of what metal was used, the hull would weigh up to 8,000 pounds. A projection had to be made as to how much syntactic foam would be needed to make the sub buoyant on the surface and also neutrally buoyant underwater so that it would not sink into the ocean floor.

Syntactic foam is a material created by using hollow spheres made of glass that are bound together with a polymer resin. Though the foam itself is heavy, the ceramic spheres provide buoyancy. It is the only material that could create enough buoyancy for a multi-ton sub while also not being crushed by pressure.

The hull and the foam would have to withstand 16,000 pounds per square inch of pressure, the equivalent of 290 fully fueled 747s stacked on top of it. Several types of steel came under consideration, including duplex stainless, nickel-rich steel, and Inconel (an oxidation corrosion resistant material), as did titanium. Any metal was believed to be better than glass because metal is more forgiving under pressure. If metal were to fail as the depth increased, it would do so slowly and constructively, rather than suddenly and potentially catastrophically like glass. A metal sphere would also be easier to build from an engineering standpoint.

Ramsay began to explore the various metals. "I am not opposed to using titanium, steel, or possibly even aluminum for the pressure hull and realize that it all comes down to cost," Ramsay emailed Vescovo on June 2, 2015. "The reason I specifically mentioned titanium was because of its high strength to weight ratio, but that's not to say it would lead to the best value solution."

Still, titanium was the most attractive solution for several reasons. For starters, its properties are well known, and it is half as heavy and twice as strong as carbon steel. In addition to strength, titanium doesn't corrode in seawater. A further factor was that the price of titanium had dropped by two-thirds over the past ten years.

Another advantage was that a titanium hull could be built without any welds. Two large pieces could be machined and bolted together. The steady increase in pressure as the sub descended would seal them tighter. This was important because welding introduces dis-continuities into the material that ultimately create localized stresses that could undermine its strength. The fact that Triton could build a spherical hull and precisely bolt it together to the required, incredibly tight tolerances rendered titanium the winner.

Triton began to delve into other major aspects of manufacturing. Two additional keys to the sub were finding high-voltage batteries that would power its systems and the syntactic foam that would be wrapped around the hull to provide buoyancy. The batteries would need to withstand the pressure and be able to deliver a substantial amount of power to the electrical system and the thrusters that would propel the sub. It was an estimated eight-hour round trip to the bottom of the Challenger Deep, not counting the time spent exploring the bottom.

Triton turned to Ron Allum, who seemed like an ideal collaborator. Based in Australia, Allum had designed and built James Cameron's *Deepsea Challenger*. He and Lahey had worked together on several projects, and Lahey considered him one of the best sub designers. He owned a company that manufactured batteries and syntactic foam.

Vescovo paid for Jones, Lahey, and Ramsay to fly to Sydney, Australia, for a five-day "sub summit" with Allum.

The meetings were productive, and the Triton team came away encouraged. Allum had insight on what needed to be improved on from the *Deepsea Challenger* to build a sub that could do hundreds or even thousands of dives over decades, rather than just one. His recommendation was to use Titanium Grade 23 for the hull. Though it would be more difficult to forge and machine than other grades, Grade 23 had a lower oxygen content than most grades, a quality Allum believed would make it more durable.

In the weeks after the summit, Allum started pressure-testing his batteries and syntactic foam, but it wasn't long before red flags popped up. The cost estimates for Allum's batteries and foam came in far higher than Triton wanted to spend. But Lahey said the real problem was that Allum's lawyer insisted that he could not provide any warranties for the components, even if they failed because of defective workmanship. Lahey pleaded with Allum to provide the warranties, but he wouldn't budge.

"We were always a little concerned that he was a one-man show who didn't have much external support, and his financial position wasn't very good," Jones says. "The thing that really killed the deal for us, though, was that he wanted to charge roughly $1 million for batteries and $1 million for foam, and he wasn't willing to guarantee it at all. We couldn't risk our client's money without a warranty."

Jones called Vescovo and filled him in. "Ron is trying to build his retirement on you," Jones quipped.

Triton would have to find other suppliers for these two critical elements and proceed without Allum. Nevertheless, Vescovo felt confident enough with these initial findings to move forward with a comprehensive design plan and cost analysis.

Vescovo had already formed a corporate entity named Caladan Oceanic LLC for the venture. He named the company after the ocean home world of the Atreides clan from the science fiction novel *Dune*, his favorite book, as he was now building his own unique ocean world, so to speak. So, the sub, the support vessel, and all financial and legal activities for the project would happen under the umbrella of Caladan Oceanic.

Vescovo brought two trusted advisers aboard Caladan, first attorney Matt Lipton as general counsel, and later a chief financial officer, Richard (Dick) DeShazo.

Lipton met Vescovo when they were classmates in the seventh grade at St. Mark's School of Texas. The two grew up near each other in a middle-class neighborhood in North Dallas and forged a lifelong friendship.

As an attorney, Lipton had counseled on several projects over the years for Vescovo's private equity firm, Insight Equity, and also for Vescovo personally. At the time he began working for Caladan, he was living on a vineyard two hours from Dallas with his future wife, trying to grow the winery and sell the brand.

"Victor is the type of person who will come to me and say, 'I'm buying a helicopter in Canada. Can you paper it, complete the transaction, and get it through customs to Dallas?'" Lipton says. "That type of thing is somewhat normal for him."

But Lipton wasn't quite sure what to make of Vescovo's plan to have a submarine built to dive to the bottom of the five oceans. "He did the seven summits and skied the poles to test himself, but other people have done that," Lipton says. "This was different. No one had done it. It was a challenge of adventure, technology, and business skills. I call him the most interesting man in the world, and I thought, if he can pull this off, then maybe he really is."

As the process ramped up, Vescovo hired Dick DeShazo to be CFO. The project was certain to be complex financially and also have its rough edges. DeShazo was brought on both for his financial acumen and his even-keeled demeanor.

A 66-year-old Southern gentleman with an accent to compliment his upbringing, DeShazo downplays his CPA credentials, such as the fact that he holds a master's degree from Birmingham-Southern College and has been chief accounting officer of a New York Stock Exchange company. He often quips that he's the product of a public school education, including his undergraduate degree from Auburn University.

DeShazo had been hired by Insight Equity in the summer of 2009 as CFO of Allied Energy Company, a fuel distribution company based in Birmingham, Alabama, near the town where DeShazo lived. The company went through some difficult times during the oil price crash of 2008–2009, but it was eventually turned around and rolled into Emerge Energy Services LP, which was taken public in May 2013.

DeShazo stayed on for two years, commuting to Dallas, and then retired in 2015. Two weeks later, Vescovo brought him back to run due diligence on a division of the company that was being sold to Sunoco. That lasted until August of 2016 when DeShazo retired again—until Vescovo called a few weeks later.

"Victor said, 'I have personal project, would you like to become involved?' I replied, 'I don't need to think about it, just sign me up,'" DeShazo recalls. "He is the smartest guy I've ever worked with. He's got the latest chips running between his ears, I'll guarantee you that. But what people don't understand is that he is 'regular people' at heart."

On August 10, 2015, Vescovo and Triton entered into a formal Design Services Agreement (DSA). Under the eight-page agreement, Triton agreed to perform the design tasks necessary to fully define the vehicle, provide a cost estimate for manufacturing, and a time frame that the company felt was realistic to engineer the world's first submersible commercially certified to full ocean depth. It would also begin to research possibilities for a ship to carry and deploy the sub, as well as planning an around-the-world expedition to the deepest points of the five oceans. After the completion of the plan, pegged at 180 days, Vescovo could elect to proceed or abandon. For this, he agreed to pay Triton $910,000.

"I was pretty sure they could do it, so this was really a down payment and 'earnest money' to show Triton I was real and to kick this off—and make sure the sub would come in at a somewhat reasonable cost," Vescovo says.

Lipton, who negotiated the agreement with Triton on Vescovo's behalf, found himself on uncertain ground. "Quite frankly, I'm not sure we knew the full extent of what we were getting into," he says. His words would be prophetic.

CHAPTER 4
LIMITING FACTORS

The search for a magical alchemy in the design of the full ocean depth submersible began in the head of John Ramsay. The 35-year-old principal design engineer for Triton Submarines was tasked with conceiving something that no one had ever done. For him, it represented the kind of challenge that he had always wanted, and one that did not intimidate.

As a kid growing up in the UK, Ramsay loved building models. He would spend hours in his room, drawing contraptions that could sail, fly, or traverse land. He followed his childhood passion to the University of Glasgow and the Glasgow School of Art to pursue a degree split between product design and mechanical engineering.

While earning the dual degree, he forged an understanding of how the aesthetics of design and the technical aspects of engineering coalesced in unique machines. However, he found that true visionaries in their fields had something of an X factor that could not be taught in a classroom.

"University just wasn't for me," he says. "I'm not sure that I found it all that relevant. To be honest, I'm not really sure you can teach design.

Engineering, yes, but not design. By design, I mean a plan or drawing produced to show the look and function or workings of something."

When he entered the world of submarines, Ramsay found a field that had few design experts, and an industry that was, in many ways, a blank page. Unlike the modern automobile industry, where designers make generational refinements to a very well-defined package, sub builders were free to make their own way and to color outside the lines. Without any "industry standard" starting point, designers were free to make revolutionary leaps forward in the vehicle's configuration.

Ramsay, who began designing submersibles for Triton in 2006, doesn't regard a sub as an esoteric subject or a mystery that needs to be solved. Where others see the marvels of technology that allow a man to ride inside a bubble immune to water pressure, he sees something much more simple that allows him to start the design of every sub, regardless of its complexities, in the same place.

"A sub is a pressure-resistant shell of some sort with people, life support, and electronics on the inside, and a chassis, buoyancy systems, and thrusters on the outside," he says. "Nothing is that crazily complicated. It's just a difficult exercise of packaging. You start by defining what goes into the sub, then arrange everything to make it as comfortable, lightweight, and compact as possible in a package that meets all of the performance requirements. Then, you progressively commit to more and more aspects of the design as parts enter production and close in on the final design."

Still, the full ocean depth submersible commissioned by Vescovo, which would be aptly named the *Limiting Factor*, would be far different from the previous subs that Ramsay had designed. The primary concerns were that it be able to withstand the pressure at the bottom of the deepest ocean repeatedly, communicate with the surface, and go down and come up in a timely manner. Other requirements, such as being able to see outside, aesthetics, comfort, endurance on the bottom, underwater speed, and stability on the surface during recovery, were all secondary.

"On a normal 3,300/3, you have to make it comfortable for billionaire passengers who want to have a drink, eat sushi, and relax while marveling at the sea life," he says with utter sincerity. "You are thinking about optimizing their view, surface stability, and making the sub appealing to look at. With the *Limiting Factor*, it was about boom!—depth—getting there and getting back. It was so pure in its objective."

Holding all of the elements of the final machine in your head simultaneously is the gift of a virtuoso designer, and Ramsay was known for his ability to do just that. His process was a bit unorthodox. Before drawing anything, he formulated a vision of the submersible in his imagination as to how form would follow function and vice versa.

"The first job is to think and think, and then think some more about aspects you know will be problematic, and to build up a mental understanding of where you are going so that it is second nature to what you are trying to achieve," he explains. "It's not a conscious thing of making a list and checking things off. You start by building up this mental understanding of what you are going to have to do to make it work before you can even really start to develop the concepts."

The centerpiece of the sub, a titanium hull, would be negatively buoyant, as opposed to the acrylic-hulled subs that Ramsay had usually designed for Triton, which were positively buoyant. This meant that the sub would have to be much taller to accommodate enough syntactic foam for buoyancy, as the hull would weigh several tons. However, the drawback of a tall sub was it would rock on the surface, so that needed to be considered.

Pressure was driving virtually every design element. The hull and everything placed outside of it would have to withstand full ocean depth pressure of over 16,000 pounds per square inch, and be designed to distribute the stress equally at ambient depths. The extreme pressure dictated that the oxygen tanks would have to be inside the hull because even the strongest oxygen bottles would likely implode below 3,000 meters. The surfacing weights on the bottom of the sub needed to release electromagnetically. Cables on the outside operating those would need to be in oil-filled junction boxes to prevent corrosion.

Over the course of two months, a vision of the submersible bounced around in his head constantly, whether he was sitting in his office or walking through the supermarket. When Ramsay felt he was close, he sat down and sketched out a few drawings.

He sent the drawings, along with preliminary mathematical calculations, to the Triton manufacturing and operations team in Vero Beach. The two sides started going back and forth over the workability of the design and discussing modifications. After each conversation, Ramsay would alter the design.

"I spent weeks working on a design that would satisfy all the concerns," he says. "But I finally realized that there was something fundamentally wrong about the design, so I had to try and take a few steps back and try and reconsider everything."

His primary frustration was that every design

had an overhang because the blocks of syntactic foam needed for buoyancy were larger than the hull, and thus overhanging at the bow, creating a feature like the peak of a baseball cap over the hull. The advantage of this arrangement was that the sub could move forward much faster. The drawback was that overhang restricted how close the sub could come to view underwater features because the viewports were beneath the overhang. The overhang was also acting like a large fin, restricting the vehicle's streamlined shape for vertical movement.

As he thought on the problem, Ramsay decided to make a compromise: *Viewing would be more important than forward speed.* He reasoned that if he backed off the concept of the sub traveling like a forward-moving train car through the water and twisted the image of the train car sideways, then he could produce clean views from all the viewports, which would be placed on one side rather than in the front. The two pilots would sit facing the viewports. This also allowed him to put the thrusters, the propellers that would move the sub through the water, on the front and back ends, rather than on the sides.

There would be ten thrusters in all. Four thrusters would be used for transverse maneuvering and rotation, essentially driving through the water, and two additional ones for slow-speed maneuvering in tight spaces. The four others would be vertical thrusters used to slow the sub's descent and for vertical control.

"After months of developing traditional frame concepts to protect the thrusters from entanglement risks, I had the idea to make the thrusters ejectable, something that, as far as I knew, had never been done before," he says.

This design breakthrough with the new configuration also resulted in other gains. Even though a tall sub would not be very streamlined as it drove forward through the water, it would have an elliptical profile that allowed for greater speed on both the descent and ascent. The "up" and "down" time was a key factor because the sub would be traveling as far as seven miles in each direction. Also, the arrangement had a relatively streamlined profile from the side, allowing the pilot to traverse significant distances during the dive.

Ramsay sketched the revision. It looked like a large pillow placed upright. The three viewports at the bottom made it appear as if the sub had a face with a high forehead above the eyes. When Patrick Lahey first saw it, he joked, "It has a face that only a mother could love."

The blocks of syntactic foam would be placed *around* the hull. The main ballast tanks would be on top. Before descent the tanks would be full of air to keep the sub buoyant; and affixed to the tanks would be electric pumps that would fill the ballast tanks with water to sink the sub. Between the ballast tanks was a tube through which the pilots would enter and exit the pressure hull. The ten thrusters, angled in different directions for upward and downward and forward and backward propulsion would go on the port and starboard sides of the sub. The batteries would be placed outside the pressure hull, tucked in between the large blocks of syntactic foam.

"I pretty much felt I had it," he says. "It all went back to the simplification concept. If you have a shape that is symmetrical side to side, front to back and top to bottom, then you can focus on designing one-eighth of the shape of the sub, because everything is mirrored. Having a symmetrical arrangement also makes manufacturing less complicated since you can use the same parts on both sides of the vehicle."

Ramsay designed the thrusters, batteries, and manipulator arm to be ejectable in the event the sub needed to make a fast emergency ascent, or if they became entangled, one of the most serious dangers to a submersible.

After Ramsay finished his concept of the design, the process shifted to what Triton needed to commit to in the near term and what could be pushed off until later. Triton began searching for suppliers for the key elements such as the titanium, the batteries, the syntactic foam, and certain hard-to-manufacture electrical components.

It was an exhaustive process that spanned the globe. The titanium was found in North Carolina. The batteries would be built in Barcelona with elements that came from South Korea. Trelleborg, a Swedish company with a manufacturing operation in the UK, was contracted to make the syntactic foam.

After six months of each department weighing in, Lahey pulled everything together and reached the point where he was confident that Triton could build the sub. He put together the multimillion-dollar cost estimate for the sub that he believed was within the upper range of what Vescovo indicated he would fund. The estimate included spares of everything—foam, batteries, thrusters, electrical circuitry—in case of a failure when the sub was on the ship at sea. It also included a $500,000 line item to commercially certify the submersible, as Triton would work hand-in-hand with the certifying agency DNV-GL and its inspector Jonathan Struwe to ensure that the necessary commercial safety guidelines were met at every step of the way.

Lahey, Bruce Jones, and Vescovo then hammered out an agreement whereby Triton would build the sub at cost, without any markup. The company would receive major bonuses for meeting certain benchmarks including commercial certification and completion of the expedition. If the sub were sold after the expedition and, depending on the price, Vescovo agreed to pay Triton above the raw manufacturing cost. Vescovo also agreed to contract Triton's personnel, at cost, to operate the launch and recovery of the sub during the expedition. He negotiated these terms hard with Triton because he believed he was putting up 100 percent of the funding, with no guarantee of success, and that Triton would gain significant brand and marketing value from a successful completion of the mission.

Vescovo also required that all parties to the project sign strict non-disclosure agreements (NDAs) regarding the project. If there were major setbacks, he didn't want himself or Triton to spend precious time or energy explaining to others what was going on. His own experience with extreme technology development had trained him that it was best to conduct bleeding-edge development in stealth mode. In that way, the team would not be held hostage to artificial deadlines or the scrutiny and negative comments from outsiders.

Under these terms, Vescovo green-lighted the construction of the *Limiting Factor*. He had plenty of experience in complex projects. For example, just one of the five companies he was chairman of at his private equity firm was an electronics service company that manufactured high-reliability semiconductors for the aerospace and defense industries. Another firm where he was chairman machined high-strength metals, and yet another built high-end defense munitions like laser-guided rockets and subhunting sonobuoys. But his time was limited and he was not an expert in submersible construction. He needed someone—not affiliated with Triton and an expert in subs—to serve as his eyes and ears as the submersible was built.

During the design phase, Lahey had introduced Vescovo to Paul Henry "P. H." Nargeolet, a legendary figure in the submersible world. In September 2016, Vescovo met with Nargeolet in New York and hired him on the spot. He was pleased with Nargeolet's input on the design, so he retained him for the construction period.

Born in France and living in the U.S., Nargeolet, who turned seventy in 2016, had done more than 150 sub dives, including thirty at the *Titanic* wreck. After serving for twenty-five years in the French Navy and rising to commander, he ran the French government's deep diving program and was in charge of the deep submersibles, the *Nautile* and *Cyana*. He developed a reputation as the guy to call for a tough deep diving mission, such as the 2009 search for the Air France flight that crashed in the Atlantic Ocean. Almost unbelievably, he had helped lead a team that found and retrieved the aircraft's black boxes on the very bottom of the ocean.

"I had been involved in some amazing projects, but for me this was truly unbelievable," Nargeolet says. "It would be a breakthrough for deep ocean diving."

The first step in construction of the *Limiting Factor* was to build its titanium hull, the sphere that the pilots would sit in. Vescovo and Ramsay had an extensive review of metals and mutually concluded that titanium would be the best bet, for workability, stability, and cost.

During a meeting in Hamburg, Ramsay met with Struwe and a metallurgist at DNV-GL to discuss the grade of titanium that should be used. They even reran calculations with some steel-based alternatives to make sure they had the strongest and lightest material for the hull.

They reaffirmed the strength-to-weight ratio advantage of titanium over steel. A titanium hull would weigh less, meaning less syntactic foam would be needed. Less foam would mean the submersible would be smaller and thus easier to store, launch, and recover on a support ship. The open question was what *grade* titanium to use—there are numerous grades, each with different characteristics, costs, and trade-offs.

Based on Ron Allum's recommendation, Triton had originally planned to use Titanium Grade 23 for the pressure hull material. But after taking advice from DNV-GL's pressure vessel experts and metallurgists, Ramsay revised the material specification to the more readily available Titanium Grade 5. He concluded that it was easier to work with and actually offered slightly better mechanical properties.

"Easier manufacturing of the hull is not the only benefit to titanium," Ramsay says. "Its relatively low density allows the hull to be exceptionally thick without being overly heavy. On externally loaded pressure vessels, thick walls are great. They are almost immune to buckling—the 'Coke can effect'—and, for our application, the additional thickness afforded by the titanium provides a great support for our eight-inch-thick viewports." All previous full-ocean depth submersibles had had just one viewport; at Triton's insistence in the pursuit of a scientifically useful craft, Vescovo had agreed to three.

Ramsay also knew from discussions with the Woods Hole Oceanographic Institution that the spheres of the *Alvin* submersible had issues with the welded joints of their pressure hull. After careful study and review with DNV-GL, the decision was made that there would also be no welds on the hull of the *Limiting Factor*. Instead, the hull would be held in place using an alignment ring and bolted brackets, with the ocean pressure itself providing the final sealing of the two halves of titanium. This also removed the need for post-welding heat treatment and eliminated any porous or other flaws in the welding that could fail over repeated dives to full depth and back. A lower-tech bolting of the two hemispheres turned out to be the best answer.

The viewports posed a major challenge. They would be made from acrylic, which is far more flexible and nowhere near as strong as titanium. In fact, the pressure placed on the acrylic would technically be higher than the rated strength of the material. Based on Ron Allum's viewports for Cameron's *Deepsea Challenger*, Ramsay created conical openings for the eight-inch-thick viewports with a slightly flexible seal around them so that when the sub descended and the pressure increased, the viewports would literally be pushed into the opening, thereby keeping them sealed.

Using titanium also allowed Ramsay to increase the size over Allum's design on *Deepsea Challenger*, which employed a single-person, quite small steel capsule, without any increase in the vehicle's weight. This was a directive of Jones and Lahey, who had convinced Vescovo that a two-person sub had far better onward sale potential than a single seater.

But the size of the hull was restricted. The first issue was that it had to fit inside a pressure testing chamber for certification purposes. The second was that the hull could not be more than 1,500 mm, or 59 inches in diameter. Export controls were placed on any vehicle above 1,500 mm, classifying them as military grade, meaning that a hull above that size would not be able to freely move from country to country. This meant that the two seats and all the necessary electronics and controls would need to fit inside a sphere less than five feet wide.

Ramsay addressed the tight space by angling the two seats slightly toward one another and putting the console with the joystick control in the middle. The oxygen bottles, allowing for a normal use of sixteen hours of oxygen with emergency supplies that could last ninety-six hours, were placed around the top of the capsule, along with carbon dioxide scrubbers under the two seats that would allow the occupants to breathe the same air over and over again.

"The life support system is obviously critical," Ramsay says. "It is designed to operate like a small, enclosed planet Earth, though without the plants!"

When the design was finally locked in, an around-the-world production adventure began. The hull was forged in February 2018 at ATI Ladish in Milwaukee in a dramatic firestorm with titanium mined in North Carolina. The spheres were then shipped to STADCO in Los Angeles and then to Spain, where they were machined to within 99.933 percent of true spherical form and the holes for the viewports were carved out. The viewports were made in Germany and then shipped to Barcelona for testing. Many electrical components for the communications system would be sourced from the UK or hand-built in Triton's facility in Florida.

To satisfy the DNV-GL safety requirements, all components of the submersible including those placed outside the hull had to be pressure tested to 1.2 times full ocean depth (20,000 psi). Working with the battery supplier, Triton developed not one, but two high-pressure testing chambers in Barcelona of different sizes for the components outside the sub, such as the batteries, cameras, thrusters, and electrical connections. Testing the hull was more challenging.

The pressure hull of *Deepsea Challenger*, though not commercially certified, had been tested at Penn State University, but that chamber was too small to hold the titanium hull of the *Limiting Factor*. The only pressure-testing chamber in the world that was large enough was located at the Krylov Shipbuilding Research Institute. Unfortunately, it was in St. Petersburg—Russia.

This posed significant challenges, of transportation, but also of politics. Given that the

Russians weren't exactly trusting of the U.S., there was a concern that the Russian government might not believe this was a private enterprise, but rather a government or even military venture in disguise. At the time, the U.S. was also in the middle of numerous government investigations into Russian meddling in the 2016 presidential election. Overall, relations with Russia were not exactly warm. What if the Russians seized the sub capsule as some form of retribution, or even just to extract a hefty "exit tax" on the now-FOD-certified capsule?

It was a chance that had to be taken to obtain certification. The 8,000-pound hull was shipped to Triton's facility in Barcelona, where final assemblies of the viewports, penetrator plates, and hatch were done. The hefty yet precious cargo was then loaded on an enclosed truck and driven 2,200 miles through five countries to the Krylov Institute.

Lahey and Struwe flew to Russia to supervise the testing and brought a translator with them. When they entered the Krylov facility, they were a bit unnerved. Rather than the high-tech sub testing lab that they had envisioned, the facility was a relic of the Cold War, a relatively run-down building with vines growing through its crumbling walls.

The hydrostatic testing chamber, named the DK-1000, was a massive underground tank.

Before placing the pressure hull assembly in the chamber, the Russian crew connected a pipe to the sub's hatch and filled the hull with water to test for any leaks. This was done because if the hull were to fail in the pressure chamber, the shock wave would take out the entire building.

The two men watched nervously as the crane operator lifted the sub from its crate and maneuvered it into the testing chamber. As the hull was lowered into the chamber, it barely fit—to the point that it scraped the sides. Lahey briefly closed his eyes.

Once the hull was in the chamber, one of the techs connected a pipe into a fitting to fill the chamber with water. Lahey thought to himself, there is no way that fitting will hold with all that water blasting in there—yet it did.

The chamber then simulated an actual dive by gradually increasing the pressure on the hull for three hours on what would be the sub's descent, holding it constant for two hours to simulate the sub on the bottom, and then reducing it over the next three hours on what would be the sub's return to the surface. The process was repeated three times, taking a day and a half, but was completed fairly quickly so as not to draw too much attention to it.

Despite working on this somewhat mysterious U.S. project, the Russian testing team was rooting for success. When the gauges indicated that the hull passed the final time, the lead technician clenched his fist in the air and proclaimed: "Da!"

The pressure hull assembly performed like a rock, with no change in stress at any of the points. At the bottom depth, it was pressure-tested all the way to DNV-GL specifications of 14,000 meters, or 45,920 feet—roughly 1.2 times the depth of the Challenger Deep. The tests validated the design, as well as Triton's calculations and analysis of the entire pressure hull assembly. At a later date, the syntactic foam blocks that would attach to the hull would be tested the same way.

After the pressure hull assembly was removed from the chamber and drained, it was repacked for transport. It would be sent by air freight to Miami, and then trucked to Vero Beach. Lahey personally sealed the container in Russia and watched it leave the building.

A week later, Lahey apprehensively opened the crate the morning it arrived at Triton's warehouse.

"Man was I nervous when I opened it," Lahey says. "For all we know they could've moved that crate to a warehouse and shipped us a couple tons of rocks."

Thankfully, the pressure hull assembly was in the crate, intact, unharmed from the journey, and now fully tested to commercial safety standards.

Triton had built a mock-up of the hull out of fiberglass and foam to determine the ergonomics.

It also built a frame out of wood to determine how the foam would attach to the hull. Using the fiberglass hull, the team set about figuring out how to assemble the electrical system and other interior components. They needed to determine the placement of every component from the seats to the electrical controls to the joystick that operated the sub. The builders would later lament that the sub sure looked great from the outside, but like the Lamborghini it was often compared to, it could be a devil to service.

The electronics were being designed and built by Tom Blades, Triton's principal electrical and systems design engineer. A soft-spoken, unassuming electronics whiz, Blades had come aboard Triton two years earlier. Both he and Ramsay worked out of the UK.

One of the challenges Blades faced was designing a communications system different than others he had done. The shallow diving subs had an ultra-short baseline system (USBL) to communicate with the surface that used acoustic pulses, but that system would not work in Hadal Zone depths. For the *Limiting Factor*, Blades would need to design a system for the sub to communicate with the ship using a modem that could transmit and receive analog communications as well as data. It would take seven seconds for sound to travel through the water column from the ship to the sub at full ocean depth. The modems Blades designed would have a time reference synchronized to the GPS on the ship, allowing Blades to calculate the speed of the sound through the water and thus determine the sub's depth.

The sub would need to communicate with the three landers dropped to the ocean's floor for navigational and scientific survey purposes. Landers are metal-framed, square scientific platforms with syntactic foam for buoyancy and weights to make them sink to the bottom. They are equipped with high-definition cameras to film the sub and sea life, bait traps to capture sea creatures, and depth and water salinity gauges. The landers required separate electrical systems to communicate with the ship's command center so they could be released from the bottom.

Blades also needed to design the control panels inside the sub that held gauges measuring depth and position, along with the monitoring and warning systems for oxygen and CO_2 levels. There would be two Toughbooks, the panels (or graphic user interfaces, GUIs, as they were usually called) used for data readout inside the sub, including the descent rate, the heading, the speed, and the depth. His approach was to duplicate each system and make them run on separate electrical circuits in the event that one of the sides, each of which contained three batteries, failed.

As the other components began arriving at the shop in Vero Beach, Ramsay was making constant refinements to the design based on functionality and practicality.

"Everything that came in was bigger than it was meant to be so you end up crowding the things into the sub," Ramsay recalls. "Tom and I used a virtual layout to study placement of the gear. We ended up putting much of it behind the seats."

The syntactic foam came in four large blocks weighing 1 ton each, with two additional blocks weighing 600 pounds each. Because the blocks were so large and heavy, how and in which order to attach the blocks to the hull became an issue. Their order determined how other components, such as the batteries and the surfacing weights, would be affixed.

Next came the positioning of the low pressure pumps that would pump out the water from the trunking that led to the hull's hatch when the sub surfaced. The final plans didn't allow enough room for them, as they were slightly larger than anticipated. More questions popped up. Where would the oil-filled electrical junction boxes be mounted? Where would the electrical wires be run? How would the batteries fit?

As the team began assembling the parts to the *Limiting Factor* in the spring of 2018, it felt like they were working on a toy model kit—without the instructions. Others likened it to a game of "submersible Tetris." "You can draw a picture and put a stickman in it, but the reality is much different," says Kelvin Magee, an experienced sub builder who runs Triton's machine shop. "We quickly figured out the sub couldn't be put together, or serviced on a ship, the way it was designed."

As Ramsay explains: "Ninety-eight percent of everything we produced was assembled, accessed, and serviced exactly as designed, which as you would hope, goes completely unnoticed. Of course, that leaves 2 percent of things that are not quite right, which then take up 98 percent of the time for the person who was to fix it—resulting in the entirely understandable misconception that nothing works!"

CHAPTER 5
CLASSING UP THE SHIP

The USNS *Indomitable* had a romantic history. Commissioned by the U.S. Navy in 1985, the ship was designed to hunt submarines during the Cold War. After its surveillance days ended, the ship was re-tasked to track down drug smuggling boats in the Caribbean. The ship was then transferred to NOAA, renamed *McArthur II*, and converted into an ocean research vessel. In 2014, a private marine company in Seattle purchased the ship and renamed her *Ocean Rover*. That was where Bruce Jones and Patrick Lahey found the ship in the spring of 2017 and targeted her, in an ironic twist, to deploy and support a sub rather than hunt them.

The Triton partners had encouraged Vescovo to finance a "turnkey" operation, which meant purchasing a ship to carry the *Limiting Factor* and its operating team around the world. They had cautioned against leasing a transport ship, as James Cameron had done with the *Mermaid Sapphire* during his 2012 expedition, because the expedition team wouldn't have full control of the vessel.

The expedition would span some 40,000 nautical

miles and take a year, perhaps longer. In addition to the vast distances between the deepest spots of the five oceans, the expedition needed to separate by six months the trips to the two polar regions, the Arctic Ocean in the north and the Southern Ocean, to coincide with the summer in each region, thus ensuring the most favorable weather. Purchasing a vessel was deemed the best option, both for scheduling and for pairing a ship with the sub to create a system that would be more attractive to a buyer.

Vescovo agreed with their assessment, reasoning that leasing would make them beholden to the ship's owner and would also provide potentially crucial flexibility if something went wrong with sub, ship, or weather. "Deep down, I said how much more would I pay to have ultimate flexibility," he says. "Bruce and Patrick told me the ship was going to cost $5 million total, about the same to lease versus buy."

After Jones and Lahey viewed a number of ships online and a few in person, they felt that the *Ocean Rover* looked like the best option. Lahey called Rob McCallum, a longtime friend who runs the Seattle-based EYOS Expeditions, a company that plans and manages maritime and other expeditions around the globe, and asked him to take a firsthand look at the ship.

McCallum, who had worked on ship builds and refits, was serving as a sounding board for Lahey as Triton developed its relationship with Vescovo, though he was not yet part of the project. "When Patrick first called me, he said, 'I've found our unicorn,' " McCallum says.

McCallum was happy to help. He jumped in his car and made the short drive to the Lake Washington Ship Canal, where the ship was moored. He toured the vessel and came away with several concerns.

"The ship needed to be reclassed as a civilian ship because the standards for military vessels are lower, and that is expensive," he recalls. "Another concern was that the lifting gear wasn't heavy enough for the size of the sub they were building. The biggest concern was that it was in really bad shape overall. What I liked was that it was built strong and was quiet, but it needed a lot of work. I told Patrick not to buy it, or to buy it with his eyes wide open."

Jones and Lahey decided it was worth a closer look, so they flew to Seattle to see the ship.

Built in Tacoma, Washington, the ship is one of twelve stalwarts; its class was contracted by the U.S. Navy, six of which were built in Tacoma and six in Mississippi. The three-deck ship is 224 feet long, with 44 berths (expandable to 49), and carries 228,000 gallons of fuel. It is powered by four diesel generators that provide electrical power to drive the propellers, which have flexible rubber mounts to dampen the engine's vibration and make it a more effective sub-hunter.

Jones and Lahey liked many things about the ship. As a naval "hunting" vessel, it was exceedingly quiet, essential for underwater acoustic communications between the ship and the sub. The ship had both a dry lab and a wet lab. The dry lab could serve as mission control and house all the communications equipment. The wet lab would serve the science team as it recovered and examined marine life.

The ship had ample outdoor deck space that could be built out for operations. The stern had a large space where a climate-controlled hangar could be built to house the submersible. This was important not only for protecting the submersible from the elements during transit, but also to give the sub crew a covered area to work on the sub in extreme weather.

Though the engines had 100,000 hours on them, they were deemed in good condition. The ship was ice classed, meaning it was rated to travel through the iceberg fields of the Southern and Arctic Oceans, also a must.

But changes were needed. There were two cranes, a fixed A-frame crane on the rear of the ship and a hydraulic knuckle boom crane that swung out over the water. The A-frame would be used to launch the sub, while the knuckle boom crane would launch the tenders and the landers (the scientific platforms). The knuckle boom crane also needed to be able to recover the sub if the A-frame failed, meaning that it would need to be upgraded to hold a 12-ton sub. While that was doable, the A-frame posed a greater challenge. Because the A-frame was fixed in place, there was an issue with how far it extended beyond the stern over the water.

Jones voiced his concern of the crane's reach. "I remember quite clearly standing on the aft deck with Patrick and saying, 'This A-frame is not long enough. It needs to be extended and beefed up because you can't recover the submarine reliably in heavy weather this close to the stern. You are going to have problems with it banging into the ship.'"

Another drawback to the A-frame crane was that it was not "man rated." This meant that the sub pilots would need to board the submersible on or over open water. But neither Jones nor Leahy saw this as a problem, as most of Triton's subs were built this way, and John Ramsay had designed the full ocean depth sub accordingly.

Lahey did an extensive survey of the ship. Other issues seemed workable with refinements. The cabins needed updating, as did the galley and dining area. The bridge also needed several upgrades. All things considered, Jones estimated the refit and renovations would cost about $2.5 million—a number that McCallum warned Lahey privately was far too low. Jones, however, was confident he could make the aggressive number work because he himself would oversee the refit. He and his wife, Liz, were also planning to live on the ship and serve as expedition leaders.

"It seemed to us to be the ideal ship from the very beginning," Jones says. "We believed that if you didn't go crazy and start to rebuild everything and redo the interior that it was in good shape. I don't know that we looked at anything after that."

Once they had settled on the ship, they were introduced to Kyle Harris, a marine diesel engineer, through a client in the Pacific Northwest. The client recommended Harris because of his local knowledge and extensive experience. Lahey and Jones invited Harris to come on a sea trial on Lake Washington to observe the ship in action. The sea trial did not go well. Harris recalls several systems malfunctioned and alarms were constantly sounding.

"Let's just say that the ship needed a great deal of work to make it functional for an around the world expedition," Harris says.

Nevertheless, Jones and Lahey liked that it was ultra-quiet, fuel efficient, large enough to hold a support team, ice classed, equipped for science, and had a large mission deck. They both agreed that the positives outweighed the negatives and that it could be made ready for the expedition.

Based on their recommendation, Vescovo

purchased the ship on March 14, 2017, for $2.5 million. The purchase of the ship turned out to be a decision that was not fully and properly vetted. The budget for the refit of the ship, set at just over $2.5 million by Jones, would fall far, far short of what was needed. The decision not to upgrade to a man-rated A-frame crane would later be second-guessed to the point that it threatened to bring the entire expedition to a grinding halt.

"When you looked at it on paper, everyone agreed that it would work fine," Vescovo recalls. "We talked about a man-rated crane, but Triton said it would be $2 million and that we didn't need it. John Ramsay got involved and said, 'We'll use this A-frame to launch and recover, and we will enter the sub from the ocean.' When you are sitting in an office looking at it on paper, of course that works. But when you go out in reality with two-meter waves, it doesn't work as well. The problem is that Patrick and Bruce, despite all their experience, had never refit a ship before. And it is a very uncertain, black art."

With the submersible in the building stage and the ship purchased, Vescovo named the venture the Five Deeps Expedition, later adding the motto "In Profundo: Cognitio" (In the Deeps: Knowledge). He combed the pages of his beloved science fiction novels to name the submersible, the ship, and the support boats, and ended up turning to one of his favorite authors, Iain Banks, for inspiration. The worlds created by Banks in the Culture series had left an indelible impression on Vescovo, and he would use them for the real life expedition he was creating.

Vescovo also saw a nice parallel to Elon Musk's SpaceX venture. Musk, also a devotee of the Culture series, had named three of his rocket-recovery drone ships after spacecrafts from the Culture series: *Just Read the Instructions*, *Of Course I Still Love You*, and *A Shortfall of Gravitas*.

"As a tip of the hat to both the late Mr. Banks, as well as Mr. Musk, who is sending things *up* while we are sending things *down*, I decided to draw on the Culture series in naming the ships of the Five Deeps Expedition," Vescovo explains. "Science fiction propels forward thought, and makes curious people want to build the things that authors have dreamed up. Our effort to reach places no one else has reached would require engineering and imagination."

After considering the many options from Banks's series, he settled on the names that were the most fitting and self-explanatory to the tasks of the vessels of the Five Deeps.

The submersible was named the *Limiting Factor*, owing to the fact that its design focused on what the limiting factors of the oceans were, notably extreme depths and how to survive there.

The ship would be the *Pressure Drop*, as it would transport the *Limiting Factor* and drop it into the extreme pressure of the oceans' depths.

The ship would carry four boats, each serving a different function. The fifteen-foot protector boat, which would be deployed each time the sub dived, would independently monitor the *Pressure Drop* and the *Limiting Factor*, triangulating communication during the dives. Its name would be *Learned Response*. A standard Zodiac boat would transport the sub pilots to and from the sub, as they would be boarding while the submersible was in the water and linked to the ship by a tether. In keeping with the "z" sound, it was christened *Xenophobe*.

The rigid-hull supply boat was named *Little Rascal* because it, well, *looked* like a little rascal and would be running to and fro with supplies. The rescue boat was named the *Livewire Problem*, because, Vescovo figured, it would likely only be used in the case of a major human error, or "livewire" (as opposed to software or hardware) problem in engineering-speak.

The three landers deployed for science and navigation were named for a major set of Culture characters—AI drones that are extremely intelligent and very symbiotic with the humans they interact with, and who also name themselves. Their full names were Fohristiwhirl Skaffen-Amtiskaw Handrahen Dran Easpyou, Sprant

Flere-Imsaho Wu-Handrahen Xato Trabiti, and Uhana Closp, which were shortened for simplicity, thankfully, a crew member later remarked, to just: *Skaff*, *Flere*, and *Closp*.

The *Limiting Factor* being the expedition's primary vehicle, it carried the designation DSV, for Deep Submersible Vehicle. The *Pressure Drop* was given the designation Deep Submersible Support Vessel, or DSSV.

"Victor always loved the game *Dungeons & Dragons* and now he had something near his own version of that," his attorney and childhood friend Matt Lipton said. "How many people get to name the elements of an oceaneering expedition?"

In no time, the budget Jones had drawn up for the refit to the newly christened *Pressure Drop* was tossed out the window, and the refit team began winging it. There were so many unaccounted-for items that costs began to escalate at a rate faster than even weekly revised budgeting could keep up with.

The main issue driving up costs was "reclassing" the vessel from a military to a civilian-owned ship. Because the vessel was built in the 1980s by the U.S. government, it did not have to adhere to any regulations set by SOLAS (Safety of Life at Sea Convention), but to reclass the vessel as a civilian research vessel, those requirements needed to be met. Triton had grossly underestimated the amount of changes that would be required to go from one standard to the higher one.

The list was long and would take far longer to complete than Jones had anticipated. The ship was not up to the fire code required on civilian-owned vessels. All of the doors needed to be changed to modern, fire-rated ones. The structural insulation on all three decks, which was non-fire retardant and flammable, had to be removed and new, fire-rated, structural insulation had to be installed—an undertaking that would take two months and a massive amount of labor.

The electrical penetrations—exposed electrical cables running through the bulkheads and decks—needed to be enclosed. Steel plates had to be placed around the cable bundles that ran from deck to deck in the stairways to prevent fire and smoke from moving between decks in the event of a fire. In total, more than fifty plates needed to be fabricated and installed, with each one taking more than 200 man hours to complete.

Safety issues also had to be addressed. The ship needed new life rafts as well as their launching cradles and stowing brackets. All of the safety gear and lifesaving and firefighting equipment had to be purchased, tested, and certified. The motorized rescue boat and its launching davit were not SOLAS-approved, so a new boat needed to be purchased, which alone cost $300,000. The communications system was also antiquated and its satellite dish, network system, and virtually all other communications gear needed to be replaced or at the very least upgraded.

"It became apparent really quickly that the refit was going to cost millions more than expected," Harris says. "Once the sale went through, we realized the amount of due diligence that had not been done."

Vescovo was, as one would expect, not at all pleased. He blamed Jones and Lahey's inexperience with ship refits and lack of communication about the potential pitfalls. McCallum was in "I told you so" mode. But at the end of the day, they were stuck with a ship that needed a lot of work.

Further complicating matters and driving up costs was that the *Pressure Drop* was being reflagged from the U.S. to the Marshall Islands. The Marshall Islands has the third-largest ship registry in the world because of its favorable regulations. Flying under the Marshall Islands flag comes with all of the protections of a U.S. ship without the legal requirements regarding international crews and wages. However, reflagging the ship meant that every aspect of it would need to be reinspected and recertified by the Marshall Islands authorities.

Part of the problem was that Jones was supervising the refit from his home in Idaho, rather than on-site in Seattle, and communicating remotely with Harris, who was handling the day-to-day oversight. Jones had never undertaken a ship refit like this and was admittedly out of his depth. To make matters worse, he underwent a four-level spinal fusion during the refit. Because he was hanging on to the project as a career capper, he pushed through and attempted to continue supervising the work during what turned out to be a longer-than-expected recovery period.

During this time, Vescovo's company, Caladan Oceanic, was hit with a $1 million workman's compensation claim. A worker fell into a hole in the deck that he claimed he had previously reported, though there were no witnesses to his injury and—in Vescovo's view—the confined nature of the area made it extremely unlikely someone could "accidentally" fall there. Vescovo blamed Jones for not paying close enough attention to the project, and not arranging for proper insurance to cover the cost of the legal defense and any claims. In fact, there was no insurance to cover this incident. Jones countered that he expected Caladan to have purchased insurance as it owned the ship and was paying the workers.

With the bills piling up and the refit running behind, Vescovo began looking for someone to replace Jones. Vescovo was put in touch with a former Navy SEAL from Florida who had done several ship refits. He hired the SEAL on a day rate and flew him to Seattle to assess the project. Lipton and Dick DeShazo, the Caladan CFO, also flew in for the meeting. Lahey met the group at the ship, along with Kyle Harris.

"It was a shit show in a good way because all the shit came out," Vescovo says.

From the ship, Lipton called Vescovo during the meeting and told him the situation was much worse than expected. He also said that it would head down a rabbit hole if the Navy SEAL were hired. Not only was the cost estimate the SEAL gave more than ten times the original budget, the man's arrogance rubbed everyone the wrong way. "This guy is a bigmouth," Lipton told Vescovo.

Vescovo needed a solution, not a further problem. The expedition would require the group to work closely together, and he was being careful to choose his team accordingly. Vescovo told Lipton to end the meeting immediately and send everybody home. He needed to think through what to do.

"I needed someone I trusted to do oversight so I put Matt in charge of general oversight, which also turned out to be less than ideal because as much as I know he wanted to help, he was understandably in a bit over his head because he had never done a ship refit either," Vescovo says. "The big point is that Bruce and Patrick made the ship refit sound very perfunctory and easy because they were hanging their hats on the fact that it was class rated. But it was class rated to *military* specifications but not modern commercial standards of the Marshall Islands flag. When there is a change of ownership, you shift to the latest class ratings. Bruce and Patrick didn't anticipate that. A big mistake that could—and should—have been anticipated."

By this point, Jones and Vescovo were on the outs. Jones was unhappy with the way things were going on the project, and Vescovo had lost confidence in Jones.

Jones acknowledges the class issues but claims that Vescovo's desire to have a more comfortable ship led to increased costs. "The refit started to grow," Jones says. "What we originally agreed on started to change, and that's not an uncommon thing with Victor. There were things people were concerned about that I wasn't. Looking over our shoulder all the time were Dick DeShazo and Matt Lipton. They are not marine guys. They don't know anything about ships. I think they were concerned that my attitude was a little cavalier."

By default, Harris ended up in charge of the refit, with Vescovo personally taking on the role of oversight, because after all, it was his money. As his girlfriend Monika said to him when he groused about the problem, "There's an old Albanian saying: 'Only the master can get his own donkey out of the mud.' "

Though Vescovo had searched for a less expensive alternative, Harris was the most practical choice, as he was already on the job. Harris had never run a full refit project, but Vescovo was impressed by his attention to detail, work ethic, and directness. Vescovo wanted the bad news immediately and the truth always, and Harris was the type of straight shooter who delivered just that. At this point, Vescovo reasoned, those qualities were actually more important than alleged "experience."

Despite the original plan to move the ship to Florida where labor costs were cheaper, the refit was forced to continue in Seattle. The ship was literally stuck in port until both SOLAS and the Marshall Islands' inspectors signed off on all the changes and provided proper documentation to satisfy the American Bureau of Shipping (ABS), the classification society for maritime safety that had a reputation for being extreme sticklers for regulatory compliance.

By this point, there was no budget. Harris was working item by item.

"Triton's budget proposal was not a realistic figure for the project, but they were fairly set in their ways that they had come to the right choice at the right price point," Harris says.

He would round up multiple bids for each item and then discuss them with DeShazo. The two talked three or four times a day. Once a vendor was chosen, DeShazo would wire payment the same day, as the only way to build credit with vendors was to pay everyone immediately.

The ship was finally certified as seaworthy in early February of 2018, and the Marshall Islands flag was raised. On the stern, where a ship displays her home port, the *Pressure Drop*'s stern displayed its home port as Majuro, M.I.— ironic as the ship had never been there. A quickly cobbled together crew sailed the ship down the west coast of the U.S. through the Panama Canal and up to Houma, Louisiana, a Cajun port town where the work could be continued at a far lower price than in Seattle.

The crew, which included Jones's son Sterling, had been pieced together by Jones from referrals. Days before arriving in Houma, the crew got wind that they would be dismissed when the ship arrived, as a new, full-time expedition crew was being assembled. This shouldn't have been a surprise, as they were not guaranteed work beyond the transit. However, they did not take the news like professionals.

Harris, who had flown to Houma, boarded the ship the morning that the transit crew departed. The vessel was trashed. There was garbage everywhere, broken bottles on the upper deck, toilets overflowing, and rotting food in the trash cans and freezer, which had been unplugged.

Without the new crew on-site, Harris hired the shipyard workers to clean and sanitize the ship so that he could resume work on the refit, yet one more unwanted cost.

Over the next four months, the extensive refit continued in Houma under Harris's direction, who had relocated to the Bayou town to oversee the work. The sewage tanks, fuel tanks, and water tanks were all pumped out and cleaned so that the vessel could go into dry dock, the process of removing it from the water. This allowed the exterior to be sandblasted, primed, and painted, and the propellers to be repaired.

An entire new control system was installed and the bridge was updated. Originally, the ship was only able to be steered from one position, in the middle of the bridge. New steering stations were added on the wings of the bridge and in the rear. This would allow the captain to see the water from all angles when launching and recovering the sub. Miles, literally miles, of new electrical cable were laid for a new control system.

During the refit, Vescovo flew his jet down to Houma to check on the status. As a former navy commander that had spent many months at sea himself, he was shocked by the poor condition of many parts of the vessel and the overall quality of the lodgings and mess for the crew. He gave Harris the green light to the make the ship livable. After all, the expedition team would spend several weeks at a time, and sometimes as long as a month, on board.

The ship has three main decks and was expanded during the refit to forty-nine berths. The upper deck houses single cabins with private bathrooms used by senior crew, the owner, and the expedition leader, as well as the captain's office. Moving toward the back of the ship outside of the main deck, there is a boat deck, housing the tenders, storage lockers, lifeboats, and emergency equipment.

Below the main deck is the forecastle deck. At the front are several cabins on either side of the hallway. Each cabin has a naval-style metal bunkbed, two metal wardrobe lockers, a metal dresser, a desk and a sink with medicine cabinet. Flat-screen TVs were added to the wall at the foot of each bed with an extensive menu of movies. Small portal windows provide a view of the water. A combined shower and toilet area is shared with the adjacent two-person cabin. In the rear of the forecastle deck is the expedition office, science office, and a large dry lab used for all the communications monitors. In back of that area is the wet lab with sinks and refrigerators for scientific research. The door at the rear leads out to the bi-level aft deck that holds the submersible and the cranes.

The main deck, a flight of stairs down from

the inside of the forecastle deck, has additional two-person cabins with connecting bathrooms, as well as one four-person cabin, the kitchen and dining area, food storage lockers and freezers, a TV lounge, the hospital, and a small gym. The entrance to the engine room located in the bowels of the ship is also on this level.

The bridge containing all the ship's navigational equipment is above the main deck. On the top of the bridge, accessible by an outdoor staircase, is an observation deck that would be dubbed the "sky bar."

During the refit, all of the cabins received new flooring and sinks. An expanded reverse osmosis water system was installed, as the existing water tank of 17,000 liters (4,490 gallons) was insufficient to keep up with anticipated consumption on a fully manned ship. The counters in the mess area were replaced and the galley was completely rebuilt to increase the number and comfort of the seats. And finally, a high-end coffee maker that produced espresso and lattes was purchased and installed. Even though Vescovo himself didn't drink coffee, he knew from his navy time that on any ship, high-quality coffee was essential for morale, if not actual effectiveness.

In early June, as the *Pressure Drop* refit continued and the departure deadline approached, tensions ran high in the shipyard in Houma. Harris and the new relief captain, Mike White, who would be part of the expedition, were at odds. Part of the conflict stemmed from the fact that both felt they had control of the ship, Harris because he was running the refit and White because he was the captain.

Things came to a head on June 6 when the *Pressure Drop* left Houma for Fort Pierce, Florida, where the final work, including adding the communications system, would be completed and the sub placed on board. As the ship sailed out of the winding canals of the Louisiana Bayou, it scraped the bottom. The mud and silt clogged the ship's "sea chest," the intake reservoir that draws water through it, and the ship ran aground. Without proper water intake, the cooling system of the engines shut down automatically and most power was lost.

"We had a local pilot, and between him and the captain the two of them decided not to follow the vessel in front of them, which was also a deep draft vessel, and go their own way," Harris says.

A tugboat had to be hired to pull the ship out of the mud. After an eighteen-hour delay, the ship was finally on its way to Fort Pierce. In the grand scheme of the rush to mount the expedition, it was more of a minor headache than a migraine. Vescovo had been so absorbed with the refit of the *Pressure Drop*, he was only just beginning to

127

appreciate the darkening storm clouds appearing over the submersible's production schedule. By this time, in nearby Vero Beach at Triton's facility, the bigger issue was that the struggle to finish the *Limiting Factor* had begun to resemble a Sisyphean task.

CHAPTER 6
TEAM LEADERS

Bruce Jones viewed the building of the *Limiting Factor* and stewarding the Five Deeps Expedition as the swan song of his maritime career. He had been waiting for the opportunity to be part of a world's first in the submersible game, both for the achievement and the notoriety. Moreover, his family would also be a part of it, as his son, Sterling, planned to be on the ship as part of the Triton crew, and he and his wife, Liz, would serve as expedition leaders. The real capstone for him, however, would be using one of Triton's contractual discretionary dives to dive with his wife in the *Limiting Factor* to the bottom of the Challenger Deep, a place only three men had gone, making her the first woman.

But this was not Jones's party, so to speak, it was Vescovo's. In its submersible construction contract with Vescovo, Triton initially had two discretionary dives at the Challenger Deep, but Vescovo took one away as part of a business transaction. Experiencing a cash shortfall, Triton asked Vescovo for a short-term, immediate $1 million loan to bail them out of a deal with billionaire Ray Dalio, who had done several projects with Triton. Vescovo agreed to lend the money, in part because the last thing he needed was for Triton to be financially unstable.

As part of the terms, Vescovo reduced Triton to one discretionary dive. Jones felt it was punitive; Vescovo called it part of a business negotiation that allowed him to reallocate the costly dive for another—likely scientific—purpose. Either way, Triton, which repaid the loan in full with interest, was now down to one dive. Unbeknownst to Vescovo, however, Jones was still hanging on to the notion that he and his wife would dive the Challenger Deep. It was, after all, in the contract that Triton would get a dive.

In actuality, Vescovo was tiring of having to deal with Jones on any front. He attributed the millions of dollars of cost overruns on the ship's refit to Jones's lack of experience. He also had let go the ship's captain that Jones had recommended in favor of someone with more direct submersible launching experience. Most of all, however, Vescovo evaluated businessmen based on their ability to manage deadlines and costs well, and Jones had done neither. It didn't help that personality-wise they were very different: Jones was a person who enjoys the good life while Vescovo was, as Lahey described him once, "a Vulcan." By December 2017, it was mutually agreed that Jones would step aside as expedition leader in favor of an experienced professional in the field.

"With Bruce, it just seemed to me that he was way out of his areas of expertise, and seemed to care more about enjoying the expedition—almost like an intense cruise—and becoming famous for the expedition, than the hellish daily grind it would take to make it happen successfully," Vescovo said. "It was quickly becoming clear that Bruce had given me really inaccurate projections, was failing at what he was responsible for, and I'd made my living off quickly changing out leadership that wasn't working out. So . . ."

However, Vescovo agreed that Jones would continue to lead the formulation of a marketing plan to find an onward buyer for the submersible and the ship since marketing seemed to be his real passion. Triton was heavily incentivized to sell the sub, as the company could possibly receive a significant, formula-based commission based on the total system sale price—if it sold. But even here, Vescovo was highly skeptical of Jones's strategy. "He said, 'We'll get a bunch of billionaires together on the ship for beers and sell it to the highest bidder,' " Vescovo recalls. "Like, good luck with that strategy . . ."

"Look," Jones says, "we were all very bullish about the future sale of the system because it is so unique."

Patrick Lahey, Triton's co-owner, was well

aware of the tension. He was caught in a tricky position between his partner of ten years and his most important client, all while overseeing the team that was building the sub.

"I'm the peacemaker," Lahey says. "That's a pretty common role I play with my partner. Bruce is a very opinionated, strong-willed person. Sometimes that ego can be in direct conflict with our clients, who also have pretty big egos. He and I have always had a stormy relationship. For me, the situation was deeply frustrating and disappointing on many levels. I'm from the school where the client is always right. Our customers—and Victor is no exception—have very high expectations, and I've learned what it takes for us to achieve those."

In this case, it was agreeing to sideline his partner from Triton's biggest project.

To lead the expedition, Lahey suggested Rob McCallum, a veteran expedition leader who had been serving as a confidential sounding board for Lahey for two years—and who had recommended against purchasing the ship for the exact reasons that were now causing the rapidly escalating costs. In late December, McCallum flew to Dallas to make his pitch to be expedition leader and to deliver him some costly news.

Rob McCallum is nothing if not experienced in dealing with high net worth individuals seeking adventure. In 2003, after a 25-year career with the National Park Service in his native New Zealand, McCallum worked as a technical adviser for the United Nations in Papua New Guinea. McCallum then started a new career in commercial maritime expeditions. He had been part of the *Mir*'s dives to the *Titanic*, and he had worked extensively with James Cameron on his ocean expeditions and as the coordinator of the test dives of the *Deepsea Challenger.*

At the time he met Vescovo, McCallum's company was operating sixty expeditions a year, including twenty-five to the Antarctic, mostly for billionaires who are tired of normal family excursions and want a legacy experience. In all, the firm he cofounded, EYOS Expeditions, had run some 1,200 expeditions.

"Our motto is that if it doesn't break the laws of physics, then it's only a matter of time, money, and another bottle of red wine," he says. "If you can imagine these things, then there must be a way."

McCallum was impressed with Vescovo's commitment to dive the five oceans. Serving as the expedition leader would only solidify EYOS's reputation as the go-to company for a complicated expedition. But McCallum had to walk a fine line; he had to explain the cracks he saw in the current plan while also trying to establish a relationship with Vescovo. He was

wary of coming on too strong and too critical of
Triton. However, he needed to be upfront, not
only to gain Vescovo's trust, but also for his own
sake if he were hired as expedition leader.

"I knew things were not going well, and I don't
think that Victor knew about how badly they
were going," McCallum says. "I was trying to
get across to him that I am not a bad news bear.
I am someone who is always truthful and here is
the truth."

McCallum laid out the problems one by one.
The operational budget that Jones had drawn
up needed to be doubled. For openers, it did
not include fuel for the ship or travel for the
Triton team that would run sub operations. He
told Vescovo that the ship's crew needed to be
replaced again with a more professional one. The
plan to have one cook on board and to expect
everyone to clean their own cabins and rotate
doing the laundry was not workable. Finally,
he said, the proposed itinerary was simply not
operationally possible.

Vescovo listened and absorbed what McCallum
was saying. The meeting at a sandwich shop in
Dallas lasted less than an hour. At the conclusion,
Vescovo asked him to prepare a new budget and
itinerary, and to recommend a new captain.

"Victor is a careful analyst," McCallum says.
"He is extremely clever. And so by showing him
where things were going wrong, he was quick to

understand the problems and also trust me to tell him the truth."

McCallum prepared a detailed document of all the things that he felt needed to be addressed, both with the ship and the schedule. He recommended Scotsman Stuart Buckle, who had actually been James Cameron's captain during his 2012 Challenger Deep expedition. He also recommended Vescovo partner in some way on the science component of the expedition with Oliver Steeds of Nekton, a nonprofit ocean research organization that had worked with Triton's subs.

A month later, Vescovo and McCallum met again. Satisfied with McCallum's new projections and his overall philosophy, Vescovo signed a contract with EYOS to lead the expedition.

McCallum made the introduction to Buckle. Before the ship's transit to Houma, Buckle flew to Seattle to see the ship—about which he had his doubts—and to meet with Vescovo. An easygoing Scot with red hair, Buckle came to the project with the ideal credentials. Having worked in the ocean and gas industry, he had fifteen years of experience deploying vessels from ships in the world's most remote regions.

Though the pay was less than what Buckle could earn on an oil and gas boat, working for a private owner had its advantages. He was allowed to handpick his crew, and he would only need to captain the ship on the dives, as a transit captain would sail the ship from ocean to ocean. Like McCallum, he was concerned about the ship, though McCallum had cautioned him not to get into a discussion about it with Vescovo.

"When Rob called, he told me, 'I have a job for you that you are not going to be able to say "no" to.'" Buckle recalls. "However, he cautioned me not to be too negative about the ship because it was too late to replace it. It wasn't an ideal vessel in terms of its age, fitness, power, and ability to deploy the sub, and it was in terribly bad shape. But I felt that with the right people in place we could get the job done."

Less than five minutes into the interview, Vescovo decided to hire the master mariner. "It was immediately clear to me that he was one of those guys that was very, very good at what he did and was also a solid leader," Vescovo later said.

Among McCallum's other concerns that he expressed to Vescovo were that the film production team Vescovo had hired were positioned to have too great a role in the expedition. To have a detailed and accurate video history of the expedition, Vescovo had signed a contract with Emmy and BAFTA award–winning documentary producer Anthony Geffen, who runs the London-based Atlantic Productions, one of the most prolific producers of nonfiction content in the world. Vescovo agreed to grant media exclusivity to Atlantic to secure a broadcaster for a series on the expedition. His primary goal was to ensure that there was a first-rate program made to document the expedition. With all the refit overruns, Vescovo also didn't want to add even more costs merely to film the expedition. Finally, he thought, someone else was willing to write some big checks.

Vescovo had met Geffen through Jones in early 2017. Vescovo had heard from Jones about David Attenborough's Great Barrier Reef documentary made by Atlantic and the Triton sub that was used. He was also impressed that Geffen had produced several landmark nonfiction television productions, particularly in natural history and exploration, including a series of films with Attenborough. Geffen had a reputation for delivering first-class films and then pushing the envelope to promote them—with great success, as evidenced by a trophy case of awards from around the world in Atlantic's London office. Such a film or series could also help promote the sale of the submersible.

Atlantic Productions signed a contract with Vescovo's Caladan Oceanic in May 2017. Under the agreement, Atlantic would pay for the expenses of the film crew, with the exception of meals and accommodations on the ship, plus take responsibility for securing all funding for the development, production, postproduction, and distribution of the documentary or series. In return for Vescovo providing the platform for the series, Geffen agreed to split any back-end profits.

Geffen traveled to Dallas to conduct some initial interviews with Vescovo to build a reel that might interest broadcasters enough to fund the filming. The British filmmaker and the Texas investor found they had something unusual in common: they had both climbed Mount Everest. Vescovo had done it as part of his "seven summits" quest. Geffen had climbed it while making a documentary titled *The Wildest Dream: Conquest of Everest*, about Conrad Anker, the climber who discovered the body of climber George Mallory, who had died attempting to summit the mountain.

Back in London, the reel Geffen and his team produced evidently worked. Talks for a series on the expedition were productive, and he was able to secure multiple meetings with interested parties.

Meanwhile, the schedule was coming together. The first dive of the expedition was scheduled for early September 2018 at the Molloy Deep in the Arctic Ocean. The ship would then sail back to Puerto Rico for the second deep, the Atlantic Ocean. On the way there and back, it would pass over the *Titanic* wreck, which was off the coast of Newfoundland. No manned submersible had been to the *Titanic* since 2003, so why not dive it?

Plans were made to bring aboard *Titanic* experts and film the wreck with high-definition cameras to evaluate its deterioration. Geffen would make a separate *Titanic* film and sell it as a special.

Geffen typically presold his ideas to broadcasters so that they were involved in the editorial process from the get-go. But this project proved to be a challenge for the standard funding model. While there was interest in the story, it was proving next to impossible to actually sign on a broadcaster and secure cash funding at this early stage. The *Limiting Factor* was not yet operational, so there was no guarantee the sub could actually reach the bottom of the five oceans. This meant that Geffen would need to invest Atlantic's money to film a couple test dives that showed the sub in action. Though it was a risk, Geffen had confidence that Triton could deliver a working sub. Some of his confidantes weren't so sure.

"I kept thinking, how is this man going to achieve this and what does it mean if he does," Geffen recalls. "The more I thought about it, the more I saw it as a story of human ambition meeting technical challenge, adding to the fact that this would happen in the deepest ocean waters where no one had gone."

Atlantic had filmed in some of the most remote places on the planet in conditions that ranged from the heat and humidity in rainforests to arctic temperatures. But filming at full ocean depth posed a new challenge. "The big issue was how to get good clear footage from outside of the sub," says Ian Syder, Atlantic's head of production. "There is a level of detail when you are talking about deep sea operations which is often beyond what we do in television. Atlantic had used underwater cameras on other series, but these cameras would need to function in much deeper waters."

McCallum, however, was concerned that having a film crew on the ship at all would interfere with the core mission of diving the five oceans. He also felt that the TV company having control of all the media was not in the best interest of the expedition.

"What was not going to work was to have the whole thing led by a film production company because they are only interested in one thing—making the film," McCallum says. "I'm the Antichrist of film production because they are wanting unscripted disasters and fuckups, and I'm wanting control and calm." The drama and "reality" that made for good television was anti-thetical to what McCallum was trying to achieve.

Jones and Lahey didn't like the media deal Vescovo made because they felt it limited what Triton could do to promote the sub. Because Atlantic initially, and the broadcaster ultimately, would have de facto control of the media during the expeditions, Triton would effectively have to ask permission to release any information about the dives. "Victor made a really bum deal," Jones says.

Geffen, however, points out that it was the only way any broadcaster would sign on to the project. "What Triton failed to understand is that there are *a lot* of diverse interests involved in any expedition of this kind and caliber—not just Triton's own interest in promoting its brand," Geffen explains. "Additionally, Triton didn't understand that broadcasters require media exclusivity so as to justify their investment in filming the expedition and producing the film."

The idea was supposed to be that Atlantic (along with any broadcasters it brought to the project), Caladan, EYOS, and Triton would work together to mutually agree on press announcements relating to dives and the discoveries. But EYOS and Triton were never fully on board with the strategy, which would cause significant friction.

To lead the science piece of the expedition, Lahey suggested Dr. Alan Jamieson, a researcher and senior lecturer at Newcastle University in

Scotland. Now that the submersible would have viewing portals and a hydraulic arm to collect samples, the expedition was looking to add a significant science dimension. Conducting science was also important to Geffen, as it added an element of interest for broadcasters and ultimately viewers beyond a man doing "hero dives" to the bottom of the oceans.

"When I first approached broadcasters with the idea, one of them said, 'I'm not going to fund some billionaire's gap year,'" Geffen says, punctuating the thought with a chuckle. "There was a real resistance to seeing past the idea that some rich guy was building a toy to break a record. But when Victor committed to do scientific exploration, the interest level increased. But that interest was always subject to the sub actually working. That was the unknown."

Jamieson was one of world's leaders in the exploration of the Hadal Zone and the ocean's subduction trenches. The 42-year-old scientist had participated in more than 50 deep sea expeditions and supervised more than 250 lander deployments. He had *literally* "written the book" on the science of the very deep ocean—among his published works was the book *The Hadal Zone: Life in the Deepest Oceans*.

Vescovo met Jamieson in London over lunch and liked both his credentials and his very direct, plain-speaking personality. An affable Scot with a thick accent and dour wit, Jamieson debunked the myth that the pilots of the *Trieste*, Jacques Piccard and Lt. Don Walsh, had seen a vertebrate on their 1960 descent to the Challenger Deep. "Their portal was tiny and there was ocean dust everywhere," Jamieson told Vescovo. "I'm telling you that you are not going to find a critter down there, but if you do, I want it! That will be a big deal."

To further entice Jamieson, Vescovo offered him exclusive use of the ship for a week to conduct scientific research in the Puerto Rico Trench in the days leading up to the deep dive there.

The two also discussed the fact that no one had definitively identified the deepest point of the Indian Ocean. It was believed to be in the Java Trench off the coast of Indonesia, but Jamieson indicated there was evidence that the Diamantina Trench near southwestern Australia could be home to it. Because Vescovo was looking at installing a massive multibeam sonar to collect data and have a hydrographer map the trenches, the expedition would be able to answer that question with certainty.

Vescovo contacted Newcastle University to bring Jamieson aboard. Vescovo reasoned that the university should just "loan" him to the expedition since the institution stood to gain from Jamieson being on a potentially historic mission, but university officials asked him for over $500,000 in compensation. Vescovo laughed at the ridiculous ask and began to look for alternatives at the oceanographic institutes of Stanford, USC, and UCLA. Weeks later, the Newcastle administrators came back to him with a modest five-figure number that he agreed to pay.

Jamieson was excited at the possibilities. He planned to bring fellow scientists on board on a rotating basis, including Johanna Weston, a Newcastle PhD student focusing on the Hadal Zone, and Heather Stewart, a marine geologist at the British Geological Survey who had done extensive work on the processes shaping the seafloor.

There were several potentially groundbreaking science opportunities that were all intertwined. The sonar would allow the scientists to examine the whole of each trench. The sub cameras would record what the seafloor in each ocean actually looked like as it traversed the bottom. The cameras would also capture which sessile (nonmobile or slow-moving) animals lived at the deepest points of the Earth.

The *Pressure Drop* would carry three landers, which Jamieson would help Triton design. He planned to bring along two more of his own landers. The lander cameras would record the larger, mobile animals to see which ones were present and which ones absent in each ocean, as well as searching for new species and researching population densities. The lander traps would capture the smaller animals, allowing the scientists to study their genetic adaptation to high pressure and phylogenetic connectivity, or evolutionary diversity, between depths and between locations.

Jamieson's plan was to gather core samples of sediment and rocks from all five oceans and conduct a microbial study on them. He would then be able to determine if they were all the same, all different, or one or more were the same. This could help in writing the story of the interconnectivity of the oceans.

"It was essentially all about biodiversity across the deepest 50 percent of the oceans, and by doing it across as many depths and locations as possible, we could then disentangle things that are true on a local scale and things that are true on a global scale," Jamieson explains. "The 'bonus balls' are always new species, plus 'money shots' of rare species and hopefully even the occasional downright weird shit that the deep sea sometimes throws up."

With the team rounded out, McCallum set up a two-day meeting in April 2018 of the principals of the expedition in Dallas. At that time, neither the ship nor the sub were ready for prime time. At all. The ship was still undergoing its refit, and the sub was being built section by section in Triton's warehouse and awaiting delivery from various suppliers—many of them late—before it could be fully assembled. The expedition schedule called for sea trials of the sub in open water to be held in early July in the Bahamas so that the ship could make the early September summer weather window at the Molloy Deep in the Arctic Ocean.

Jamieson, Buckle, Jones, and Lahey all attended the meeting at the DFW Airport Hyatt Regency, along with Vescovo, his CFO, Dick DeShazo, and attorney Matt Lipton. With Geffen tied up on another project, Atlantic's head of production Ian Syder, who would be handling the nuts and bolts of filming, flew over from London. Karen Horlick, who handled logistics for EYOS was also there, as was Phil Algar, whose company had been contracted to provide the ship's hotel staff. Vescovo had not invited Nekton's Oliver Steeds as he wasn't yet sure what incremental benefit Nekton could bring to the expedition and was already feeling saturated with relationships to manage.

McCallum had T-shirts printed with FIVE DEEPS EXPEDITION on them to help make everyone feel they were part of a team. He prepared a PowerPoint presentation listing the five objectives, describing how the schedule would work, and detailing how each group served the other.

The five objectives were straightforward: to execute all mission activities in a safe and efficient manner; to reach the five deepest points of the world's oceans; to undertake further exploration dives to targets of interest, including possibly the *Titanic*, USS *Scorpion*, and USS *Indianapolis*; to generate multidisciplinary science data for the global community, and to provide outreach material that will inspire and encourage further exploration. McCallum saw the film as part of the fifth objective, far down the list.

A lengthy discussion took place about installing a sonar on the ship to map the trenches. Everyone was advocating for the sonar, as it would increase the reach of the science, provide a better explanation of the ocean floor for the film, and add value to the ship itself. The price was a hefty $1.5 to $2 million for a state of the art multibeam echosounder made by Kongsberg, a Norwegian company, a number not at all contemplated in the ship's original budget.

"I was a big champion and so was Bruce of multibeam echosounder," Lahey says. "It was the only way you can substantiate the depth, and it's a hugely valuable asset to the vessel and an important part of attractiveness to an onward buyer."

Vescovo was annoyed at this very late, seven-figure addition to the budget seemingly out of left field. While Vescovo was wealthy, it irked him how so many members of the team—especially Jones—found it so easy to spend his hard-earned money and seemed to view him as an unlimited ATM. However, he eventually agreed that the logic of adding the sonar was sound—regardless of the messenger or tardiness of the proposal. The unanswered question became when and where could it possibly be installed without interrupting the expedition, as the ship would need to go into dry dock for several weeks so it could be attached to the bottom of the ship. McCallum, who had several shipyard relationships, began to look for a solution.

All in all, the meeting was a success—except for one exceedingly awkward moment. Jones announced that he and his wife would be diving in the *Limiting Factor* at the Challenger Deep. Lahey was aware of his partner's intentions, but had been so busy with the sub he hadn't addressed it. Everyone else in the room was surprised and looked directly at Vescovo. Inwardly, Vescovo was shocked. To him it was obvious that the two "Triton divers" should be Patrick Lahey—the builder of the sub—and, okay, maybe Bruce Jones, even though he was not directly leading a core part of the expedition any longer. More appropriate would be Lahey and the sub's gifted structural designer, John Ramsay. But Jones's wife? He thought she was a very nice person, but it just didn't seem fair or frankly deserving to Vescovo, compared to others who were contributing so much more blood, sweat, and tears. Jones's feeling was that Ramsay was young and would have other opportunities, and that it was Triton's dive so they had the right to decide the occupants.

With all eyes on him, Vescovo concealed his instinctive reaction and chose not to directly address the issue at that time. He needed things to keep moving forward, and with the exception of Jones, who had been moved to a nonoperational role, he was pleased with the team that had been assembled.

"It's a rainbow coalition on this expedition," Vescovo said after the meeting. "It's all about competence. It's not about any political agenda. When you are up on Everest and it's storming, you are saying to yourself, 'I'm glad I bought the best money could buy and I'm with the best team. When I'm down there at 16,000 PSI, I'll say I'm glad I spent the money I spent and have the best team.'"

CHAPTER 7
SWEATING OUT THE SUMMER

Victor Vescovo landed his Embraer Phenom jet at the small private airport in Vero Beach, Florida, on the morning of June 20. He had traveled to South Florida with his Caladan team, attorney Matt Lipton and CFO Dick DeShazo, so they could see for themselves the progress on both the *Pressure Drop* and the *Limiting Factor*. The ship, which was docked in Fort Pierce, was nearly ready to go, but the sub, which had been undergoing assembly for three months in Triton's facility, was behind schedule. It wasn't so much that Vescovo wanted to pressure Triton as it was that he needed to begin assessing the situation. The delays in assembling the *Limiting Factor* were threatening to create a major schedule overhaul to the Five Deeps Expedition before it even got started.

The pressing issue was that the sea trials in the Bahamas to test the sub needed to be finished in early August at the latest, or the *Pressure Drop* would not have enough time to steam to the Arctic Ocean for the dive at the Molloy Deep before the weather turned for the season. Missing the weather window would add at least three months and well over a million dollars to the expedition.

Vescovo, Lipton, and DeShazo rented a car and first drove to the port in Fort Pierce where the *Pressure Drop* was docked. Kyle Harris and his team were in the final stages of the refit. The ship had undergone a total transformation since any of the three had last seen her. When they pulled up, Vescovo commented, "Look how pretty she is, all new and painted."

Harris gave them a tour of the vessel, highlighting the work that had been done and outlining the remaining items. A large satellite communications dome that would provide Internet and telephone service for the ship was sitting on the dock. Along with the servers and computers, it was expected be installed the following day and brought online by Pippa Nicholas, the English-born communications expert.

"It's a wee bit shaky at the moment, but we will continue testing it," Nicholas told Vescovo.

Nicholas was one of what Vescovo called the project's "rainbow coalition." Since being hired, she had undergone transgender surgery and now liked to flaunt her new assets. The only thing that mattered to Vescovo, however, was that she was highly competent because comms issues at sea would be problematic for him personally. He needed very robust communications with shore to maintain his business interests while at sea.

Several other issues were being addressed, the biggest being the cradle and the hangar that would house the *Limiting Factor*. Originally, Triton had outsourced the design of the cradle that would hold the sub on the ship, but that hadn't worked. John Ramsay then redesigned the cradle and the hangar so that Triton could build and machine them in-house. But even when the setup was finished, unanticipated complications occurred when interfacing the hangar with the ship. Once again, something Triton thought would be easy was not.

The science freezers were running late because of miscommunications, but Harris was pushing to have them installed before the vessel sailed for sea trials. Harris had thought Alan Jamieson, the science team leader, had ordered them, while Jamieson assumed that Harris had. "The lines of communication haven't been the best," Harris said.

Overall, Vescovo was pleased with the ship. Lipton and DeShazo agreed that it had come a long, long way since they had last seen it. In the car driving to Triton, Vescovo told DeShazo that he wanted to give Harris a bonus for pulling the ship together in such a professional manner and on such a tight timeline. "I like to bonus people who deserve it and don't ask for it," he said.

When the three arrived at Triton, the mood was upbeat and anticipatory. Lahey shook hands with Vescovo and sarcastically asked if he would like to see the sub. "Do ya think?" Vescovo replied.

Lahey led Vescovo into the warehouse. He explained how what looked like pieces of a giant model would be assembled. Huge blocks of syntactic foam stamped with "389 kg" (858 pounds) were sitting on the floor. The thrusters (the sub's propellers and their casings) were spread out on workbenches waiting to be affixed. Vertical hoppers with steel slugs weighing 50 kilograms (110 pounds) each were off to the side, as was a bound mass of massive steel bars each weighing 250 kilograms (550 pounds) that would serve as the freeboard weight, the final weight dropped to make the sub fully buoyant. At the center of it all were the bolted-together titanium hemispheres that would house the pilot and passenger.

For Vescovo, just seeing all the components under one roof after three years of planning was exciting, even though nothing had been attached to the hull and the electrical components were scattered across several tables. With childlike enthusiasm, he climbed into the sphere to check on the height of the center console and get a feel for the capsule.

Next, he moved to a workbench with the manipulator arm clamped to it. The hydraulic arm, which would allow the sub pilot to interact with the atmosphere, had been manufactured by Kraft TeleRobotics at a cost of $350,000. They were the only company Lahey contacted that was willing to work on the project. It was the company's first product rated to full ocean depth and had the power to lift 180 kilograms (396 pounds). Vescovo grasped the handle. As if he were playing a video game, with the twist of his wrist he began maneuvering the arm and picking up wood blocks the way he planned to collect rocks and other materials from the bottom of the oceans.

Lahey explained that progress was slow because the company was waiting on numerous suppliers, many of whom were running behind, and consequently every day was one step forward, one step sideways. "We started to put the sub together in March, and we are waiting and waiting on all kinds of things that are behind schedule," Lahey said. "It's ridiculous the number of things that are behind schedule."

After the tour, the group went into the conference room for lunch. The current problem in a series of them was that the sub's batteries were delayed. Ictineu, the manufacturer located near Triton's Barcelona facility, was running behind, and the batteries would still need to be pressure tested once they were finished. Cost for 10 batteries: $1.5 million. "You'd think they could pick up the pace at that price," Lahey said.

Lahey had initially told Vescovo that Triton could obtain a permit in Spain to fly the batteries to the U.S., but that didn't pan out because the batteries are made of lithium polymer, a hazardous material. The options now were a commercial cargo ship or a private ship, or transporting them to another country and flying them in a private plane. Based on cost and practicality, the decision was made to put the batteries on a cargo ship to Miami and pick them up on July 19. "It's too bad my plane doesn't have the range, or I would go get them myself," Vescovo said.

Four days later, another distraction involving Bruce Jones reared its head. His son, Sterling, was let go from the ship because there was no real role for him going forward, and the following day he quit his job at Triton. Jones sent Vescovo an emotional email. "Empathy wouldn't appear to be something you do, and it certainly doesn't appear to ever enter into your decision making," Jones wrote. "You have managed to become vastly unpopular with both my wife and my youngest son; and you hardly know one another."

Lahey, already under enough stress, decided enough was enough. Calling his partner's email outrageous, he emailed Vescovo, "It would seem I will have to make a full time job of apologizing for my partner's behavior and all I can do is assure you this changes nothing as far as my commitment to you, the *LF* project and the FDE [Five Deeps Expedition]."

Given the fractured relationship between Jones and Vescovo, Lahey had come to the conclusion that it was best Jones not come on the ship at all. He told McCallum, who passed the news on to Vescovo. "I can't see him adding anything to the project other than stress and drama," McCallum emailed Vescovo.

For Jones, the end of his desire to be a part of the expedition would come a month later when Vescovo notified him that he would not allow his wife, Liz, to dive in the *Limiting Factor* on its discretionary dive at the Challenger Deep, even if Lahey piloted the sub. He said that it was an insurance liability.

Jones felt like the rug had been fully swept out from under him by Vescovo. "If you want to get to me, start with my son and end up with my wife and then you have an enemy for life," he says, punctuating his thoughts with an uncomfortable chuckle. "Victor is a great guy and I appreciate him as a client, but he agrees to lots of things then he changes his plan at the end. Guys who operate at that level in a dog-eat-dog private equity world try and create their own reality. That was pretty much the end of our relationship."

Vescovo, who no longer had time for the drama,

says that Jones "did a series of things that showed that he not only needed to be out of the orbit, but in a different galaxy. He just hadn't delivered."

As June ticked away, the pressure on the Triton team increased as things were not coming together as planned. The fact that the company was making a first-of-its-kind submersible with no road map to rely on had become readily apparent.

In addition to suppliers running behind, every time a piece of the sub was affixed to the hull, something else had to be moved. The compensators needed to be repositioned because they did not fit in their planned locations. There was no space for all the electrical cables, resulting in the syntactic foam being cut. All the while, no one was quite sure how the batteries would fit into the junction boxes because they were still in production.

John Ramsay, the sub's designer, had relocated from the UK to Vero Beach for the final assembly phase. He was pulling his hair out over the problems. "I wasn't feeling overly optimistic," Ramsay admits. "Those last few months were utterly brutal. I didn't appreciate quite how much work had to go into the assembly and how different a new-build submersible was to what we had built before."

Admittedly, a major issue was poor project

management. "We hadn't pushed vendors early on or got on top of production well enough to make sure everyone was going to deliver in our time frames," Ramsay says. "Every vendor pushed every delivery to the very last minute. Too much came in too late to make it a comfortable build. It was just unbelievably stressful."

Kelvin Magee, the veteran head of Triton's machine shop, was accustomed to the final weeks of assembling a submersible being chaotic, but he had never experienced anything quite like this. "Everything had to finish up at once," Magee recalls. "We were problem solving as we went. The confidence level that we could get the sub done in time for sea trials that summer wasn't very high. Patrick asked me one day, 'Are we going to get this done?' I said, 'I don't know, because I don't know what I don't know yet.' "

Lahey was dealing with vendors from all over the world: the U.S., Australia, Germany, Spain, the UK, and Canada. It seemed that every time he would give Vescovo a completion date, a vendor would notify Triton they were late, forcing the date to shift. When that occurred, Triton needed to re-plan what it could work on. The company was also forced to send employees on location to work with some of the vendors. One of the key engineers, Hector Salvador, spent most of his time at Ictineu dealing with the batteries at a time he was needed in Vero Beach for the build.

On June 28, Lahey informed Vescovo that the sea trials would need to be pushed back from July 16 to July 23. By July 4, it was becoming apparent that the July 23 date could not be met either. Lahey called McCallum to tell him the situation before he delivered additional bad news to Vescovo.

McCallum emailed Vescovo that "Patrick is sweating bullets and wanted to sound me out about another delay." He asked Vescovo to keep this between them so that Lahey would continue to use him as "a safety valve and confidant to bounce things off."

Buckle, the ship's captain, was overseeing the installation of the sub hangar on the *Pressure Drop* and the delivery of the support boats. Every time he interacted with Lahey, he could feel the anxiety. He told McCallum he was concerned about Lahey personally, which McCallum passed on to Vescovo.

Vescovo pushed back. "As for Patrick's mental state, well, I have to say he brought it on himself," he emailed McCallum. "Bruce is obviously of no help, and they have just taken on too much, and with too much optimism. But I can't afford to be overly sympathetic anymore. I have a lot of people and dollars at stake here. Patrick needs to go to war and get this done."

The following day, July 5, Lahey emailed Vescovo about the further delay. He admitted that Triton had fallen short of the deadline, but also made the case that Triton was not that far behind the original timetable. He pointed out that the construction contract for the *Limiting Factor* was signed on July 18, 2016, with an expected delivery date of 24 months later, which was to include sea trials. He assured Vescovo that Triton "has pulled out all the stops" working seven days a week, twelve hours a day.

"The *LF* is an order of magnitude more difficult and the other variables including the hangar, *LF* trolley, landers, and *PD* integration together have completely overwhelmed our capacity and used up our entire bandwidth," Lahey wrote. "Add to this the need for us to fulfill our obligations to other clients, which can at times conflict with our *LF* objectives, and you can appreciate the difficulty."

Vescovo was irked because regardless of what the contract said, Lahey had promised an earlier completion date upon which the entire machinery of the expedition—and its associated high expense—had begun. Lambasting Lahey over the multiple missed deadlines, he reasoned, wouldn't make things better, however. Instead, he opted for a measured, somewhat positive response. He explained to Lahey that "planning and commitments were made based on the schedule that Triton created, not Caladan or EYOS, that had us starting sea trials in early June, so in fact even if we make the July 25th, then by my reckoning, we will have had roughly a 7-week delay, not 17 days (as sea trials was supposed to be concluded in that 24-month period). But that will all be water under the bridge if we can make Molloy and *Titanic* in the critical weather windows with successful dives."

Copied on the email chain, McCallum wrote Vescovo: "Patrick is a dear friend but he needs to learn that optimism can be expensive. He needs to stop telling folks what they want to hear . . . and tell them as it is (with a contingency buffer!)."

Lahey admits it was a "clusterfuck," but adds: "Let's not forget we were building the world's first full ocean depth–certified human occupied vehicle."

Though Vescovo continued to believe that he had hired the best sub builder in the world and contracted with a first-class film production company, he was feeling frustrated at their ability to work together. There had been a miscommunication over the cameras, which were being supplied by the Woods Hole Oceanographic Institution (WHOI). Though Atlantic had been in touch with WHOI and the Triton team, somehow the final schematic for the cameras had not been given to Lahey until the week before departure for sea trials. "This is simply not acceptable," Lahey emailed Vescovo. Not only did there need to be an allowance in the sub's design for the cameras, the inspection agency required that they be independently pressure-tested to full ocean depth—not a short time frame activity.

By the time Lahey received Atlantic's drawing for placement of cameras inside the sub and outside the sub, it was too late to install them on the outside of the sub. A discussion ensued to see if temporary cameras could be mounted with Velcro for sea trials so that Atlantic could get underwater footage to show prospective broadcasters, but the Triton team had too many other items on its list to deal with the exterior cameras.

Vescovo emailed Geffen that the cameras could not be mounted in time for the sea trials dive. Geffen said that he understood and would discuss how to deploy cameras outside the sub on future dives. Vescovo was frustrated that he ended up in the middle of the situation that should have been taken care of by both sides.

On July 12, Vescovo decided to make a surprise visit to Triton. After finishing a business meeting in the early afternoon in Richmond, Virginia, he and his copilot flew to Vero Beach instead of heading back to Dallas as planned. Unannounced, he showed up at Triton to check on the progress of the *Limiting Factor*.

He walked into the lobby of the warehouse.

Through the open door of the main high-bay, he could see the components of the *Limiting Factor* scattered around the floor, but there was no one working on the sub. The only work underway was on a different submersible.

Vescovo was not pleased. He had been promised by Lahey that the team was working twelve-hour days in shifts, breaking only for the heat. Lahey was at the facility, and the two talked briefly. Lahey attributed the inactivity to the late hour and the day's heat wearing people out. He told Vescovo that he was going to have a large A/C unit installed in the building to allow shifts to last longer. Vescovo was dumbfounded that something so necessary hadn't already been installed.

"The guys are busting their humps twelve hours a day, seven days a week," Lahey told Vescovo. "I've been burning my crew out every day. They are human beings, too. You have to let them rest."

The next day, Vescovo offered a bonus to Triton if it finished by July 25, as the financial consequences of not being ready were coming front and center. Lahey turned down the offer, almost as if Vescovo had insulted their dedication by thinking more money could make things go faster. But Vescovo had made his point: Triton needed to marshal all its resources to finish the sub sooner rather than later.

Still, on July 20 it was clear that Triton would not be ready in five days. Vescovo decided to give them four extra days and to pull back from his daily emails to Lahey. He felt that Lahey was so overburdened that any further prodding would only make things worse. He had made his point by showing up unannounced. Sometimes, he had learned, even in a battle you had to just step back and let things happen.

The batteries finally arrived from Spain that afternoon, as did the final cables necessary for other electrical connections. The last of the parts to finish assembly of the *LF* were due first thing the following morning.

"All major components now on-site," Lahey wrote to Vescovo. "It's going to be a busy weekend."

"Sounds like Christmas . . . and you even have the batteries," Vescovo wrote back.

A July budget analysis prepared by Dick DeShazo showed costs had escalated dramatically. The biggest jump was on the *Pressure Drop*. Originally estimated by Jones at $5 million on the high end, the final number was heading north of $12 million. This included the addition of the unplanned multibeam sonar to collect data to map the ocean floor, budgeted at $2 million. The *Limiting Factor* appeared to be coming in just above Triton's original cost estimates, but without substantial, customary overhead costs or any profit margin.

DeShazo estimated the total expected combined costs for the *Pressure Drop*, the *Limiting Factor*, and the around-the-world expedition to "shake down" and perfect the submersible would be over $40 million. Vescovo thought that given so much remained unknown and left to do, even that was conservative. He expected a full 20 percent more in unexpected costs would arise and that the entire system costs would end up being $50 million. To date, he had already spent more than half that amount. It was the cost of the remaining "unknown unknowns" that kept him up at night.

As the final budget numbers were being pulled together, Triton and Caladan were in the process of concluding the onward sale agreement for the *Pressure Drop* and the *Limiting Factor*. Each side was coming up with different numbers for the asking price, and there was a fluid debate over what costs would be added to the entire system to determine the sale price.

The key points had been agreed to. Vescovo only wanted to recoup his expenditures for building and perfecting the system and was not taking any profit. Triton would receive a reimbursement for foregone overheads and a minimal profit margin on the design and building of the *Limiting Factor*. If all went well, the company would independently receive from

Vescovo a total of $2.5 million in bonuses, for DNV-GL certification, a successful dive to bottom of the Challenger Deep, and completion of the Five Deeps mission, which would be included in the asking price.

Another pressing question became what to do with the expedition costs, which were rising because of unaccounted-for line items and delays. All estimates relied on the assumption that the expedition could make the weather window to dive the Molloy Deep in the Arctic Ocean in September—no sure thing because the *Limiting Factor* was still in pieces. If that window were missed, the Molloy Deep would have to be pushed to the fall of 2020. Because the expedition had been scheduled to end in May 2020 at the Challenger Deep, this would add another three to four months—a considerable additional expense.

Finding even modest sponsorship revenue to offset costs was going nowhere. Originally, Triton had estimated there could be $5 million in sponsorship income.

Nevertheless, Vescovo was comfortable proceeding, though at the same time he was trying to contain costs. In business ventures, he operated on the philosophy that if you can't control costs, everything else becomes irrelevant and you will never succeed. Uncontrolled costs equals venture failure—in anything, he had learned. Certainly, his abilities to control costs and maintain schedule discipline were being put to the ultimate test.

"Coming in 'over budget' by about 30 percent? Well, as these things go, I can't say it is a mortal blow," Vescovo wrote DeShazo in an email. "Could the U.S. government or Navy have done this for a similar amount? *No way in the world.* And why not? is the question that should be asked, and discussed. Just glad I am able to do it and hopefully we are successful."

The next headache had nothing to do with the sub. Before sea trials, Vescovo was insisting that everyone sailing on the ship sign a waiver of acknowledgement of risk and limiting exposure to gross negligence in the event of injury. He was already fighting what he deemed a bogus workman's comp claim that had occurred during the refit in Seattle.

In light of that claim, the liability waiver was particularly one-sided. Participants had to agree to personally assume all risk for injury, illness, or death, and responsibility for any medical expenses that the participants or others incurred on board the ship. The waiver further stated the participant agreed not to sue Caladan "for injuries or damages whether they arise or result from any NEGLIGENCE or other liability, EVEN IN CASES OF GROSS NEGLIGENCE."

On the eve of sea trials, John Ramsay, the

sub's designer, Tom Blades, the chief electrical engineer, and Richard Varcoe, the website designer, all refused to sign the liability waiver. When Vescovo found out, he pushed back hard, threatening to ask them to leave the ship and work remotely. DeShazo contacted Lahey, who tried to persuade Ramsay and Blades, both Triton employees, to sign the waiver, but they balked.

Faced with a decision, Vescovo decided to allow the three on the ship for sea trials and discuss the issue with them. There was simply no practical way to conduct sea trials without the sub's designer and the electrical engineer on board. He related to them his experience with a workman's comp claim already in motion, and he wanted them to commit to him that they wouldn't file another. Enough to his satisfaction, they did, and they were allowed on board.

With the clock ticking and the Molloy Deep weather window closing, Rob McCallum flew to Florida to monitor the situation firsthand. On July 25, McCallum arrived at Triton around 6:30 A.M. with bagels and coffee to check on the final assembly of the *Limiting Factor*. He felt that the tide was finally turning, and that completion was in sight.

"(The extra four days you gave them) has served to lift them out of the 'fug' and into a more positive and energized run for the finish," he reported to Vescovo via email. "There was activity in every part of the building today; with John (Ramsay) and Jonathan (Struwe, the certifier from DNV-GL) going through test protocol, Richard on the website, 4 different benches of electrical work, 3 folks working on the dummy and 6 on the fitting of lights and external hardware. The 4 days delay has been a good investment and in hindsight they were not going to make tomorrow."

Two days later, on July 27, McCallum met with the Triton department heads individually. After hearing from each one of them, he concluded that mobilizing for departure to the Bahamas the following evening was not possible and asked each one for an honest appraisal. A consensus was reached that Thursday, August 2, could be met.

An understandably impatient Vescovo was miffed. The topsy-turvy scheduling was wreaking havoc on his scheduled workload at Insight Equity. He and his partners were in the process of selling a construction company that he was chairman of and which they had owned for ten years, but there were numerous technical wrinkles. He was also in the midst of a potential $80 million purchase of a lumber company in East Texas. Complicating matters, however, was the owner. A good old boy, the man had declared that he only did business on a handshake, and thus refused to let the Insight team talk to any of his customers. With every delay, various meetings with important people had to be rescheduled.

Surprisingly to some, Vescovo hadn't even told his partner, Ted Beneski, whom he had worked with since 1994, about the *Limiting Factor* or the expedition. "He doesn't tell me what he does on his weekends," Vescovo said. He planned to break the news to Beneski the day before it became public. Another, less optimistic and darker part of him wondered if the sub would actually be built, test successfully, and the expedition ever started. He decided he would announce what he was doing to others when it was really "on."

He changed his departure plans for the Bahamas a third time. "The general verdict? Patrick is a great sub pilot and builder, but he is not the best project manager," he said. "He has a poor habit of letting his optimism get in the way of cold calculations, and leaving little or no allowances for the natural friction of business, tech development, or construction. That isn't a damnation of him, it's just that we've discovered his weakness and it is a big one that I wish I had known sooner. I could have helped mitigate it with more milestones and inspections. I should have known better when they didn't deliver the first simulator on time—it was more than a month late. People that miss schedules don't usually get a lot better at it with larger and more complex things."

August 2 came and went, and on August 3, McCallum reported to Vescovo that there was a further 24-hour delay in loading the *Limiting Factor* onto the *Pressure Drop*. The repeated delays had left no time for harbor trials in Fort Pierce, meaning that the sub would not enter the water until it arrived in the Bahamas. That violated their original plan and skipped a whole "harbor trial" testing interval.

That evening, McCallum left Ft. Pierce to run a previously planned expedition in Svalbard, Norway, somewhat ironically the place the *Pressure Drop* needed to be in less than a month. The prolonged building period was causing the expedition leader to miss sea trials. He put his capable colleague Richard Bridge in charge, but not having McCallum there was less than ideal given the intense state of play and his detailed involvement.

On August 3, the *Limiting Factor* passed the Factory Assembly Testing, an inspection conducted by DNV-GL's Struwe, who would accompany the Triton personnel to sea trials. The team had been in constant contact with Struwe throughout the design and build phases so that there would be minimal problems with certification. The next step would be for Struwe to observe the sub while it was operational and rate its capability and most importantly, its safety.

Finally, on August 4 at 11:30 A.M., the *Limiting Factor* was trucked from Triton's facility to the port in Ft. Pierce. The submersible was loaded onto the *Pressure Drop* that afternoon. As the ship sailed for the sea trials in the Bahamas, the Triton team was still doing the final assembly on the sub. "What I didn't want to happen was to finish the sub when it was on board the ship, which is exactly what happened," Triton's Magee said.

Magee had several concerns, notably the durability of one of his final-hour fixes. There had been problems sealing the trunking that the pilots would use to enter the sub and enter the titanium sphere. Magee had come up with a decidedly low-tech solution—he had used a Schwinn bicycle inner tube as the rubber seal.

"My biggest fear was that the trunk was going to leak from the bicycle tube seal," Magee said. "I also never trusted the frangibolt holding the batteries or the thrusters. Each battery packs weighs 400kg. The manipulator arm weighs 100kg."

Because of the manufacturing delays on the batteries, Triton had only the six batteries needed to run the sub and no spares. If a battery were lost or malfunctioned, the sea trials would be over.

Relieved and feeling optimistic, Lahey sent a heartfelt email to everyone involved in assembling the *Limiting Factor*, calling it the most important project in his life. In part, he wrote: "I wanted to take a moment to remind all of you that the journey you are a part of is historic. The *LF* project is bigger than all of us. This submersible promises to really make a difference and allow human beings to regularly and safely visit the deepest, most remote and least understood part of our planet for the first time in history. We should all step back, catch our breath and consider the magnitude and significance of what we are doing right now and revel just a little bit in the moment. Life is fleeting and not everyone has the opportunity to be a part of a project that can move the needle, shape or impact history and change people's perceptions forever. You all have this opportunity and I do hope you are as proud and excited as I am to play a role in this remarkable endeavor."

As inspirational as Lahey's email was, there remained a very big unknown: because the sub had never been in the water, no one was exactly sure how it would perform. Vescovo's feared "unknown unknowns" would soon surface.

CHAPTER 8
SEA TRIALS

The *Limiting Factor* wasn't performing. The shiny, white two-person submersible, measuring 15 feet long, 6.2 feet wide, and 12 feet high, weighing 25,700 pounds, or 12.8 tons, might have been a feat of inspired design, technical engineering, and electronic wizardry, but from the moment the first-of-its-kind submersible was lowered into the water, it was also clear that the *Limiting Factor* had its share of gremlins.

The sea trials were being held in the Bahamas, a couple miles off of Abaco Island. The location was chosen for the azure blue, calm waters on its westward side, a place to give the Triton Submarines team optimal conditions to test the launch and recovery of the *Limiting Factor*. Less optimal was that the owner would be one of the sub's test pilots and a film crew from Atlantic Productions would be on board the *Pressure Drop* filming them.

Rob McCallum, the expedition leader, didn't want Vescovo or the cameras near the sea trials, but that wasn't in the cards. "I made very clear that it was a high-risk time," said McCallum, who missed the sea trials because of a prior commitment. "Rule number one is you need to keep the client away from the sub until it is working as planned. But because Victor was the owner and one of the test pilots, that was the beginning of the frustration that he started to experience—'I've got this new toy, I paid a lot of money for it, I'm hugely invested in it, it's my baby, and it's not working like I think it should.'"

Normally, Triton would have ironed out the kinks before letting the client dive in the sub. And even if a film were being made using one of their subs, they wouldn't let the cameras near it until the sub was fully operational. But in this case, the client was essentially managing the entire project, which was running so far behind schedule that the expedition might have to be rerouted and extended, and the film crew needed footage to secure a broadcaster and its all-important funding.

Atlantic had six people on the sea trials. To capture the footage, it used one camera on deck, one in the tender, two inside the sub, and a drone. Additionally, a diver would use an underwater camera to film the sub descending.

Triton's Magee, who has an easygoing demeanor, was less than pleased with having a film crew on board. "We are working with a brand-new sub and a brand-new boat while TV people film us going through our learning curve," he said. "We're doing it with our skirt right up to our ears. I think having the film crew here was the wrong thing to do. We can't admit mistakes and have our usual testing process because it will end up in the film. It's not how you do things. We don't go out with our client to test his sub, and we sure as fuck don't go out with Atlantic Productions."

Vescovo certainly understood this, but was between a rock and a film camera. Without any video of the system in actual operation, Atlantic was likely to abandon the project. He would then have to fund the multimillion-dollar budget to properly film the expedition for posterity, or scrap the filming of it altogether. Neither was an appealing option, so he decided to endure the displeasure of Triton instead. It was the least worst option at that time.

Initially, Triton had planned to conduct harbor trials in Fort Pierce. This would have allowed it to practice the Launch and Recovery System (LARS) and to test other deck equipment and systems aboard the *Pressure Drop* that were directly involved in submersible operations, including the lifting winch that picked up the sub. These systems included the tag line winches that stabilized it, the towing winch, the "knuckle boom crane" that launched the *Learned Response* support boat, and the A-frame crane that lowered the sub into the water. But they had run out of time, so all of these would be tested for the first time in the Bahamas under the glare of the cameras and the scrutiny of the owner.

Lahey was tense, but trying to be circumspect about the setup. "Sometimes in the rush to completion you don't always do things the way you might have liked to do them, you do them in a way you needed to get the job completed," he said. "You make compromises as you have to, though not ones that jeopardize the vehicle's safety. Everyone knew going in that it was unrealistic to have everything working perfectly, and we would just work through them in a more public forum than we would have normally liked."

To no one's surprise, problems occurred on the first dive. Lahey piloted the sub with Magee riding shotgun. The waters were calm, the weather ideal. They dived the *Limiting Factor* to twenty meters to test its core systems. The first thing they noticed was that the main ballast tanks that were supposed to fill with water to cause the sub to submerge weren't sealing properly. This meant the sub would not descend properly.

"There are 'duck' valves that are supposed to allow water to flow in but not out," Magee explained. "They failed miserably, so we have to redesign them."

A bigger issue was the *Limiting Factor*'s

buoyancy level above the water's surface, known as its "freeboard."

The sub surfaces by dropping weights. The first weights dropped are the sixteen 5-kilo (11-pound) Variable Ballast Tube (VBT) biodegradable steel weights, which are dropped one by one about 200 meters from the bottom until the sub is neutrally buoyant. The VBT weights are housed in two long columns on either side of the pilot sphere and dropped sequentially. When the sub is ready to surface, the pilot drops any remaining VBT weights and also a single, 250-kilo (550-pound) surfacing weight which causes the sub to ascend fairly rapidly, about 2.5 feet per second. Once it breaks the surface, a large freeboard weight is dropped, pushing the sub high enough for the majority of the trunking column to be above the waterline. Most of the water in the trunking is then pumped out mechanically. After the sub is attached to the ship by a towline, before the hatch can be opened, a "swimmer" enters the trunking and pumps out the remaining water with a handheld pump. The swimmer then opens the now dry hatch so that the pilots can exit the sub.

But when the sub surfaced on its first dive, and then again on its second dive, it wasn't becoming positively buoyant, meaning its freeboard was too low. This meant that water was sloshing into the trunking faster than the pumps, or even the swimmer, could pump it out, and therefore opening the hatch was difficult. More concerning was that this was occurring in calm waters.

"The fine details of its buoyance couldn't be worked out until the sub was in the water because we didn't know exactly how much it weighed," explained sub designer John Ramsay, who was on board despite his refusal to sign a liability waiver required by Vescovo.

Jonathan Struwe, the DNV-GL certifier, was on the ship observing and offering guidance. Because of the buoyancy problems, he could only rate the sub to sea state 1, pejoratively called "mill pond" conditions. It needed to be rated to at least sea state 3, moderately rough conditions that would be faced on open water in the oceans.

The list of gremlins stacked up quickly. The manipulator arm was not operational. Semi-conductor fuses failed during the on deck start-up procedure. The starboard cameras were not working. The battery pods need to be changed too frequently. And the launch and recovery of the sub was a shaky procedure at best.

"We need to figure out how to get the thing over the stern and back on board before anything else matters," Magee said.

A side issue was that the ship's crew struggled to deploy the *Learned Response*, the protector boat that triangulated communications with the sub and the ship. The boat was launched from the second deck using the knuckle-boom crane. The process went so poorly the first two times that Captain Stuart Buckle told Lahey that the boat would have to be replaced, as it appeared that it could not be raised or lowered on its cradle in anything greater than sea state 1.

Vescovo, whose arrival at sea trials had been delayed by Lahey in hopes that the sub would be fully functioning before he arrived, took the problem in stride.

"They bought a protector boat that is just too big and ungainly to be effectively used where we are going," Vescovo said. "So now we have to figure out what kind of boat we can use effectively and maybe even have to do structural modifications to the *Pressure Drop* to accommodate a different boat or to ease launch and recovery. This problem will get solved too, but will also take time and also money—not to mention potentially $300,000 wasted on a boat I can't use."

Buckle was also concerned about the lack of safety procedures being followed. The Triton crew didn't all wear helmets, and some wore flip-flops instead of protective shoes while working on deck. At one point, Lahey was nearly decapitated by a flying metal hook. "My concern is the safety of everyone on board, and they are being very cavalier about it," Buckle said.

And only one of the three landers was operational. With so many problems, the chances of making the Molloy Deep weather window in 2019 were rapidly starting to fade.

"It isn't the end of the world," Vescovo added. "The basic design is still valid and I am confident the sub can be 'fixed,' but killing Molloy in 2018 will add another two to three months to the expedition and cost at least $1 million in crew expenses."

The good news? "Everyone says the food is great," Vescovo quipped.

The sea trials were the first time the film crew and the sub team had met one another, and the Triton team felt like it was under a magnifying glass. The Atlantic team was concerned at how many things weren't working with the sub, as other expeditions they had filmed were always up and running by the time they arrived. But all other expeditions had the luxury of precedents and sea trials conducted before the unveiling of the sub. The *Limiting Factor* was not only 100 percent new and in virgin territory, it had not even been in the water before sea trials because of time constraints.

Though both Triton and Atlantic were under different pressures, their goals were mostly aligned. Triton needed to test and troubleshoot the sub and ensure that the LARS (Launch and Recovery System) worked. Atlantic needed to film enough footage of the sub in action to convince the Discovery Channel that the sub was viable. Network executives would understandably not sign off on funding a series until they saw evidence that the sub could dive the ocean depths, which meant that Atlantic had to fund the sea trials shoot.

In an attempt to bring a production deal together quickly, Anthony Geffen, Atlantic's CEO and founder, had invited a Discovery Channel executive to watch the sea trials. Geffen, who had already been forced to eat the costs of having a crew ready twice before when the arrival of the sub was delayed, was understandably eager to secure Discovery's commitment.

Atlantic had made films of underwater exploration all over the world, including two on billionaire Ray Dalio's ship using Triton subs, but Geffen was concerned by watching the operations on the *Pressure Drop*. It took three days for the Triton team to get the sub in the water, and the results on the first dives were underwhelming to say the least.

Indeed, the Discovery executive, who watched the first two days, called the situation "chaotic." No one involved could disagree.

After receiving the reports of the problems with the sub, Vescovo finally decided he needed to see what was happening firsthand. Rather than wait until Lahey informed him that the sub was fully operational, he made plans to fly to Marsh Harbor in hopes of enough issues being resolved that he could dive the sub.

Vescovo's plan was to fly from Dallas to Jacksonville with his copilot, Manny Montes, on August 8, overnight there, and then head down to Marsh Harbor first thing the morning of the 9th.

He took off from the private airport in Addison, Texas, in the late afternoon of the 8th. Somewhere over Alabama, he and Montes were reviewing the checklist of documents needed to enter the Bahamas. One key document was missing: Victor's passport. "No, really, I'm not kidding," he told his copilot. In a hurry, he had left it in his car when switching luggage, which was parked in his airplane hangar.

With no other alternative, Vescovo radioed air traffic control that he was returning to Addison "for operational requirements," and literally turned the plane 180 degrees around at 41,000 feet. An hour later he was back on the ground in Addison. After refueling, passport in hand, he took off again for Jacksonville. The false start somehow seemed fitting.

The following morning, Vescovo and Montes flew to the tiny airport on Abaco Island. He touched down in the late morning and was driven an hour to a dock where he boarded the *Learned Response* to take him to the ship. Geffen and his camera crew were on the support boat filming Vescovo's arrival.

"I thought it would be fun to maybe be the first guy to fly a plane and dive a sub on the same day," Vescovo commented offhandedly. "How many people have done that?"

Vescovo boarded the *Pressure Drop*. Lahey greeted him and told him that the plan was to do two more practice dives that day before Vescovo dived the following day.

"I want the sub to be working and ready before you dive it," Lahey told him.

Vescovo was clearly disappointed by not being able to dive on the day he flew, but he deferred to Lahey.

The two reviewed the list of issues, which also included the battery banks not functioning properly.

"Given all these issues, do you think we will be able to do Molloy?" Vescovo asked.

"I do, barring some unexpected problems," Lahey said, ever the optimist. "The next couple days are critical."

With Vescovo observing, Lahey and Magee dived the sub. The dive was more successful than the previous ones, but there was a close call when the sub resurfaced. It came up about fifty feet from the ship, far too close for comfort. There had been a disconnect in communications between the *Pressure Drop* and the *Learned Response*. The *Pressure Drop* control room had said not to bring the sub up, but the *Learned Response* crew cleared the sub to surface.

"We popped up way too fucking close," Lahey said when he was back on board. "We need to work that out."

Several electrical problems also persisted. Lahey vowed to work through the night to correct them so that Vescovo could dive the following day.

After the Triton crew had worked through most of the night and much of the following day, the sub was ready for Vescovo to dive it. He and Lahey boarded the sub for his first dive.

The launch and recovery went smoother than the previous dives. As the sub descended, Vescovo turned to Lahey and told him, "I love the sub. Thank you."

The dive was both to test the sub and for Vescovo to become comfortable at the controls. He had spent more than forty hours working with Lahey via Skype in a simulator in his garage in Dallas. Being a fixed wing and a helicopter pilot, much of the process, like constantly checking oxygen and CO_2 levels and monitoring electrical systems, came naturally.

Vescovo and Lahey stayed down ninety minutes. Though the sub performed reasonably well, there was a laundry list of things that did not function properly. Vescovo's headset did not work, nor did the rear camera, which meant that many of the circuit boards would need to be pulled and tested. Intermittently, the sub's headings displayed on the screen did not change when the sub changed directions. One of the batteries, which has 160 volts, showed 0 on the monitor, despite the fact it was providing power. The readout on the VBT weights—those released at the bottom to make the sub neutrally buoyant so it can hover—showed they had discharged, even though they hadn't. Several alarms were also going off that shouldn't have been.

Still, back on deck, Vescovo was visibly excited by the experience. It had been 1,429 days since he had first emailed Triton about building him a submersible, and he finally dived it. "The dive was awesome," Vescovo said. "We have several things to work out, but the core systems are working."

Lahey was relieved that Vescovo finally got to dive the sub. "It has been a rollercoaster ride," Lahey said. "The team is exhausted from last three months but has also been invigorated when you actually see it happen. The sub is not 100 percent, but maybe 90 to 95 percent. We've had some big setbacks, some where people would be inclined to throw up their hands. And then we had some big victories. Now we are going hell for leather until we are over the finish line."

The biggest problem to date came to light in the ensuing hours when one of the landers failed to resurface. Two landers, *Skaff* and *Flere*, had been deployed before the dive. *Skaff* resurfaced on cue but *Flere* did not.

The landers were designed with two layers of redundancy so that they would resurface. The first means of release was actively "pinging" the lander acoustically through its modem to drop its surfacing weights. If that failed, the backup system was an "egg timer" that was set to release the weights at a certain time after launch so that the lander would resurface. However, neither release had worked. The lander was still on the bottom of the seafloor. Where exactly, no one knew. Vescovo was surprised that there had only been a double-redundant, and not triple-redundant, system on something so valuable.

A discussion ensued about what could be done to find the lander, as a new one would cost in the neighborhood of $300,000—more than the entire sea trials. Tom Blades had the coordinates where the lander had been deployed, but there was no way to know if it had drifted. Lahey suggested they dive the *Limiting Factor* and see if they could spot it. Hopefully, the lander's lights would still be working.

Lahey also got in touch with Triton client Carl Allen, who owns a 3,300/3 sub and the support vessel *Axis* and asked about using his sub to search for the lander. Allen okayed the mission. Lahey made plans to send two Triton employees, Mat Jordan and Frank Lombardo, to meet the *Axis* in the coming days and work with Les Annan, the *Axis* captain and an accomplished sub pilot, to find the lander.

That night, Lahey and Magee dived the sub again so that Atlantic could film it glowing under the water. Geffen sent a diver in the water to film the sub from below. He had also been allowed to attach temporary Go Pro cameras to the sub. After the night dive was complete, Geffen now had enough footage to cut a teaser reel.

The following day, before Vescovo departed the ship, he and Lahey dived the *Limiting Factor* again, this time to 480 meters, the deepest it had gone. The launch was dicey, and the recovery took more than a half hour, far longer than expected. The issue was that even in sea state 1, the sub rocked back and forth. While sacrificing surface comfort had been a design choice Ramsay made to make the sub faster when going up and down in the water column, in a more harsh sea state the pilots would be uncomfortably tossed around, particularly if the recovery process was not more fluid.

Ramsay was frustrated that the sub wasn't ready for prime time. "It's a bit embarrassing," he said.

By the final day of sea trials, Vescovo coldly

concluded there were just too many problems to proceed to the Molloy Deep and believe that they would be successful. The plan now was to send Triton back to Vero Beach to execute the punch list and then return to rougher and deeper water in the Bahamas for what was being called "*Advanced* Sea Trials." This would cause the expedition to miss the Molloy Deep weather window, thus pushing the Arctic Ocean deep off until the late summer of 2019. And so, before the Five Deeps Expedition had even started, it had already been extended by at least three months.

"You've got to hand it to Victor, he can take the knocks, he really can," McCallum said. "He takes the bad news well."

Geffen was pushing Vescovo to kick things off at the *Titanic*, rather than start with the first—and much closer—Puerto Rico Trench off Puerto Rico. He had tentatively sold the idea for a one-hour special examining the deterioration of the wreck to National Geographic Channel and other broadcasters, as Discovery Channel had turned down doing an additional show beyond its possible commitment to the Five Deeps series. The *Titanic* dive would be the first manned dive to the wreck since 2004 and the first that would return 4K images.

"Victor, *Titanic* is huge," Geffen told Vescovo over dinner on the ship. "It's the perfect launch for the Five Deeps."

Vescovo agreed, but weather again was the issue. Depending on how long Triton needed before Advanced Sea Trials, a *Titanic* dive would not likely be until late September, or even early October, at the tail end of the ideal time to dive there. Over the next few weeks, Buckle and McCallum weighed in. Both agreed that it *could* be done, but of course, there was no way to predict the weather off the coast of Newfoundland.

"*Titanic* is riskier in October, but we can wait in St. John's (Newfoundland) for a weather window and scamper out there," McCallum emailed Vescovo. "There is a higher chance of bad weather (Autumn is coming), but before it comes there are usually some nice calm days and settled periods. It is not ideal, but the fact is that I simply do not have any faith in Triton's dates . . . so I want to give them more space than they would ever ask for, and then work with you to drive them hard to perform and deliver."

Aside from the *Limiting Factor* not behaving during the first sea trials, the teams were operating as factions focused on their own interests, not as a single unit as McCallum had preached at their pre-expedition meeting in Dallas. The strife spilled out into the open after the sea trials ended.

Lahey was single-minded about Triton's

interests. In addition to making the *Limiting Factor* operational, he was advocating that the *Learned Response* did not need to be replaced. If it were, the cost of the new boat would be added to the expedition cost, thereby decreasing Triton's potential level of cost reimbursement. He blamed Buckle for not paying close enough attention to the launch and his crew for not rigging the boat properly.

"I watched the crew aboard *PD* attempt to launch and later recover the *Response* and it was clear they did not know what they were doing and had not thought through the process at all," Lahey emailed Vescovo. "I saw men holding lines while being catapulted through the air and slammed into hard structures on deck."

Lahey was also irked by Buckle throwing out several negative jabs about the *Pressure Drop* in front of his crew. Lahey, who along with Bruce Jones had selected the ship, was already sensitive about the ship because of the soaring costs of the refit and had taken to trumpeting its better characteristics, namely that it was roomy, had minimal acoustic noise, and was extremely fuel efficient.

"I remain concerned about the constant flow of negative comments from Captain Stu regarding *PD*," Lahey continued in his email. "He continues to characterize *PD* as an old, tired and worn out platform, which is tedious and destructive. *PD* may not be a state of the art [ship] like the other vessels Stu is accustomed to operating but she is a fantastic and capable vessel ideally suited to her current role. If Stu has such a low opinion of *PD* and her capabilities, why did he take the job of Captain?"

Vescovo asked Buckle about his making derogatory comments, which could be damaging to morale as well as the onward sale of the vessel, but Buckle denied making any negative comments and said that he would not do so in the future. As the gripes poured into Vescovo's email inbox, he turned to McCallum to be peace-maker. "Hopefully he can help short-circuit what appears to be growing hostility between Stu and Patrick," he said of his expedition leader. "It isn't helpful, like at all. Both sides keep making snide comments about the competence of the other. I personally think there is some truth to both sides, but much less than is real."

McCallum stepped into the breach as the arbiter. "Patrick is likely feeling that he's lost ground and credibility," McCallum told Vescovo, "I'll work on illustrating to him that the key to success is the success of the team. There cannot be factionalism. Not now, and not when it gets tough."

Sea trials had become people trials. In the days following the first sea trials, another tense back-and-forth email exchange took place concerning the lost lander. Theories abounded as to what had happened to *Flere* and who was to blame.

The L3 Communications team that operated the lander's modems faulted the lack of a launch checklist and said that the crew had failed to attach the power cables from the batteries to the electronics, evidenced by the fact that they had never had contact with the lander after it was deployed. While the battery-driven "egg timer" should have released without the power connection, they also said that two of the four egg timers they had used had previously failed, so they were going in with a 50 percent failure rate on the backup system. Triton was planning to return those egg timers and find new ones after the sea trials, but it appeared that the damage was done.

Lahey told Vescovo that he believed the lander had flipped over. "The terrain at the site is rocky and rather steep for a lander and it is entirely possible *Flere* struck a boulder or haystack on the way to the bottom and toppled over and headfirst into the bottom rendering the modem and release mechanisms unable to work properly," he said.

Alan Jamieson, the chief scientist, rejected Lahey's theory outright. He explained that as a matter of physics the weight and buoyancy distribution made the possibility of the square-shaped lander flipping over pretty much impossible. Despite the fact that Jamieson was supposed be in charge of the landers, he had let Triton design them. He blamed Triton's construction of the landers, which he pointed out was already suspect because the electrical board that Triton had installed in lander *Closp* was built wrong and it had fried the moment the power was turned on.

"It became apparent that nobody fired up the modem on deck prior to launch, therefore I think a dead modem is more likely the result of connector damage through water ingress the day before," Jamieson emailed Vescovo. "I can't reiterate enough that the landers cannot end up upside down or on their side, they are only 40kgs in water with loads of buoyancy pulling up and the ballast pulling down. It just can't happen."

Vescovo sat back and watched it all play out. "Patrick was afraid I was going to deduct dollar-for-dollar from my final payment for the *LF* the cost of the replacement lander, as well as the cost to extend the FDE by another two months ($500k?)," he later emailed. "Dr. Jamieson was thinking I was going to fire him. And the calming influence of Rob McCallum was out of the picture. Anyway, welcome to the circus. <wry half smile>."

A week later, *Axis* sailed to the Bahamas with Triton's Lombardo and Jordan on board to search for the lander *Flere*. They rigged a system to pull the lander out the silt if they located it, but after a day of searching for it in an acrylic Triton sub, they had no luck.

Lahey delivered the news to Vescovo and said that he had implemented a plan to build a replacement lander, dubbed *Flere²*, by the second sea trials. However, he cautioned that it would be a challenge to get the syntactic foam from the UK, a new modem, and a replacement junction box with all the required cables and connectors in such a short period of time. He also asked Vescovo to pay the expenses of the *Axis* team for the search.

Vescovo pushed back slightly before agreeing. He asked Lahey if he had offered a "bounty" for the lander in the event that it had surfaced after the ship left the area. While Abaco Island was relatively remote, the other areas of the Bahamas were heavily populated with tourists and boaters. He also floated the idea of sending his helicopter to the area to conduct a detailed, low-level search along the shoreline.

Vescovo told DeShazo and Lipton that Lahey "offered his apologies for losing the lander, but it rang a bit hollow to me, truth be told. It kind of felt like, 'Oh well, sorry about that. Please send another check for another lander.' "

He was more concerned that Lahey had gone forward with sea trials with a sub that wasn't ready. "He went to sea with major systems not operational," Vescovo said. "He is the kind of guy that looks up at Everest from base camp and thinks to himself, 'Oh, that should only take a couple of hours . . .' Inexperience and unabashed optimism is a bad mix here, but we are slowly getting a handle on it."

After the sea trials, Vescovo prepared a detailed "anomaly" list of more than fifty items that needed to be addressed before Advanced Sea Trials—"again, dragging the donkey out of the mud," he said. He put them in three categories: one for "must-have" items, two for "could-wait" items, and three for "when you can" items. Among the eleven category one items that needed to be addressed on the *Limiting Factor* were the duck valves, the VBT system, which sometimes jammed and did not release the weights properly, and multiple alarms that went off because of improper power distribution. Category two included labeling the light switches and fixing the A/C system. On the Toughbooks, category one items included fixing the descent rate, the heading indicator and the depth accuracy on the surface, as the GUI showed the sub 10 to 16 feet underwater when it was on the surface. There was a separate list for the landers. Top priority: a triple redundancy recovery system to prevent the loss of another $300,000 lander.

Lahey originally targeted August 27 for the Advanced Sea Trials, but Vescovo had little confidence that Triton would be ready by then. He told Lahey that he would not green-light a second sea trial until all the category one items had been checked off the list. The target completion date was moved to the first week of September.

On Labor Day, September 3, two days before the *Pressure Drop* was scheduled to sail to the Bahamas, Vescovo made yet another trip to Triton to check on the progress of the anomaly list. "I feel like Darth Vader going off to inspect the behind-schedule *Death Star*," he joked.

The first thing he noticed when he arrived, which slightly annoyed him, was that Lahey had given everyone the day off. Sure, it was Labor Day, but the *Pressure Drop* was just forty-eight hours from sailing back to the Bahamas for a second sea trial, which needed to be successful before an attempt was made to dive the *Titanic*. Lahey brushed it off, saying everything would be ready by launch time.

Vescovo spent nearly three hours at Triton's facility meeting with Lahey, as well as with electrical engineer Tom Blades and chief scientist Alan Jamieson, who was there to supervise the rebuilding of the landers.

Big-ticket items such as power distribution, the VBT system, and the duck valves were finished, and the Triton team was deep into the other category one items. Vescovo and Lahey did a full start-up test of the *Limiting Factor* in the shop, and all systems worked as they should. They had a "clear electronics board" for the first time. Two of three cameras were working, with the aft camera set to be installed the following day. But several analog instruments required by DNV-GL for temperature, humidity, and barometer still needed to be hooked up, and the manipulator arm was still not active.

Jordan, the Triton electrical engineer, had designed a more robust timer circuit for the landers. In addition, an 800-pound breaking strength, galvanically corroded release set at twenty-four hours would be installed as the third redundancy that Vescovo now required.

On the electronics front, Triton was also waiting for DNV-GL to approve the underwater cameras that Atlantic Productions was licensing from the Woods Hole Oceanographic Institution before installing them. There were so many electronic issues that "Blades was in 'an execution bottleneck' even though Patrick has a hard time admitting it," Vescovo said after his visit.

Lahey had been through the building and testing process many times and was sanguine about it. "I've never encountered any fucking sub project that I have done in my fucking nearly thirty-eight years of doing this stuff where it is easy right out of the gate," he said. "At the beginning, it's brutal and it's going to look like a train crash in slow motion, and that's exactly what it does look like. But eventually, you figure it out."

The *Pressure Drop* sailed for round two of sea trials in the Bahamas on September 5. A series of dives over the next three days showed remarkable improvements. On its first dive, the sub maneuvered and performed to expectations, with only a few electrical glitches. The following day, it dived to 1,180 meters. Then, on September 9, Lahey and Struwe went to 4,926 meters, a depth that ensured DNV-GL would commercially certify the sub, and a dive that showed depth wasn't going to be an issue for this vehicle. It was functioning like a tank underwater.

On each dive, the LARS team was becoming gradually more efficient at launching the sub and bringing it back on board, but there was still work to be done before heading into rough waters. "Our performance has gone from a C to a C+," McCallum told Vescovo.

Vescovo arrived on board the evening of the 9th. The relatively successful deep dive had moved the needle on the Triton's mood from frustrated to cautiously optimistic.

The following day, Vescovo dived with Lahey. They targeted 5,000 meters. The launch went off without a hitch. As the sub descended, despite a few minor issues, the two had strong communications with the ship and the dive was going well.

But when they reached the bottom, at 4,900 meters, and Vescovo turned on the hydraulic system and attempted to use the manipulator arm, it abruptly shut down. A small puff of smoke wafted through the cabin. A fire in a sub is one the worst things that can happen because it eats up oxygen rapidly, and to put out a fire the pilots either have to contaminate the air with fire retardant or take out the oxygen—both of which are harmful to humans.

Vescovo and Lahey looked at each other wide-eyed and were silent for a single, long second.

"Do you smell that?" Vescovo asked.

"Yeah," Lahey replied.

"What was that?" Vescovo asked.

"I don't know," Lahey replied.

They pulled out and readied the scuba regulators for emergency breathing and then began double-checking all systems to determine if there was any imminent danger that needed to be dealt with. There was no depth reading, as the CTD circuit responsible for providing the reading was apparently fried. The manipulator current connector also appeared to be fried, but nothing appeared life-threatening. A trained pilot, Vescovo did what any pilot would do, he undid the last thing he did before the smoke appeared:

he turned off the hydraulics. The smoke did not reappear.

They signaled the *Pressure Drop* that they were immediately aborting the dive. Swiftly, they dropped the VBT weights and the surfacing weight and headed to the surface—over an hour and a half away.

Back on deck, they breathed a sigh of relief before delving into what had happened. "While I don't think we were in danger of having an actual fire, it was a scary moment," Vescovo said. "It's those first seconds where you think, 'holy shit,' before you return to your training and work the problem."

After the biggest electronic gremlin to date, Blades set about trying to figure out what had happened. After several days of troubleshooting and consulting with other experts in submersible electronics, Blades determined that when the manipulator arm was powered on, a current was unleashed that caused a surge to escape through the CTD, an instrument used to measure the conductivity, temperature, and pressure of seawater, and shorted it out. The current became so high that the accessory circuit breaker detected the surge and tripped the circuit, which stopped the runaway current and shut down the manipulator arm. Because the current surged, it burned out an in-cabin connector to the manipulator, thus causing the puff of smoke.

Despite this event, Vescovo was mostly pleased with the progress at Advanced Sea Trials. He emailed the team a riff on the Dos Equis commercials starring "the most interesting man in the world," the bearded character in the TV ads that bore a resemblance to him. On his dive with Lahey to 4,970 meters, Lahey videoed Victor holding a Dos Equis and delivering a variation on the ad's tag line: "I don't normally dive to the bottom of the ocean, but when I do, I prefer to take a Dos Equis."

Based on the Advanced Sea Trials dives, Struwe issued a DNV-GL class certification for the *Limiting Factor* on August 13. Struwe classed the submersible to 5,000 meters with a technical capability of full ocean depth. He recommended it not be launched in sea state 4 or greater. The *Limiting Factor* was now the first commercially certified, privately owned submersible classed to 5,000 meters.

"Very well done by all involved," Vescovo emailed the team.

The news was a boost to the morale of everyone involved heading into the first open water ocean dive at the *Titanic*. Still, the fact of the matter remained that the fate of the Five Deeps Expedition ultimately hinged on the *Limiting Factor* being fully functional and launched, diving and recovered on a continuous basis in much rougher seas.

CHAPTER 9
CIRCLING THE *TITANIC*

*T*itanic. It's the iconic underwater image that evokes feelings of grandeur, tragedy, mystery, and Leonardo DiCaprio romancing Kate Winslet. While diving the *Titanic* wreck would be the first chance to test the *Limiting Factor* in open ocean waters, it was really about a splashy kickoff for the Five Deeps Expedition, as this would be the first manned dive to the wreck in thirteen years. If you were going to do an open ocean sea trial, Vescovo figured, why *not* do it at the *Titanic* if you could?

In addition to serving as a launching point, successful dives at the *Titanic* would be a boost to all involved. Atlantic Productions had the most on the line. Geffen had sold the rights to a one-hour program on the *Titanic* dive to National Geographic Channel and other broadcasters. He had also arranged a media day in New York for October 19 aboard the *Pressure Drop*, which was scheduled to sail south and port there after the *Titanic* dives, to announce the start of the Five Deeps Expedition.

Triton was organizing a smaller media event the same day for the ship community. The company held the exclusive rights to sell the ship and the sub through January 31, 2019, at a minimum price of $48 million, so it needed to begin to drum up interest from possible buyers. What better way than having its first full ocean depth sub dive the *Titanic* en route to the ocean dives?

For Rob McCallum and EYOS, it was another chance to show they were the go-to company for complex expeditions.

Having the *Limiting Factor* dive the wreck of the *Titanic* would connect people to the expedition in a way that starting out at Molloy Deep or the Puerto Rico Trench would not, because it was far more relatable. "You could go to the bottom of the oceans, find a unicorn, the lost city of Atlantis, and a spaceship, and people will more likely remark: 'He went to the *Titanic*!' " McCallum said.

The RMS *Titanic* famously hit an iceberg and sank in 1912 about 370 miles southeast of Newfoundland at the nautical coordinates of 41.7° North, 49.9° West. The wreck lies at approximately 3,900 meters, or 2.4 miles below the surface, in two main pieces roughly one-third of a mile apart. Though more than 140 people had been on dives to the wreck since it was discovered by Robert Ballard in 1985, no manned submersible had been there since James Cameron and his team dived it in 2005.

Although the *Titanic* was a British ship that

sank in international waters, and the Five Deeps Expedition was flying under a Marshall Islands flag, a U.S. federal court order was required for the dive. To help protect the wreck and prevent the plundering of artifacts, the U.S. government had placed the wreck under the governance of the U.S. District Court in Norfolk, Virginia. The Consolidated Appropriations Act of 2017 protects the wreck from being disturbed—by American citizens, anyway—and further bills passed by the U.S. Congress make removing artifacts from the wreck a criminal act. Only one company, RMS Titanic, Inc. (RMST), was authorized to remove and preserve artifacts from the wreck. From 1993 to 2000, the company conducted numerous dives and recovered more than 4,000 items, many of which were on display at their for-profit exhibit at the Luxor in Las Vegas.

Securing the permit was something of a bureaucratic nightmare. McCallum sent sixty-eight emails in relation to the application. The week before the expedition was to set sail for the wreck, three representatives from NOAA, one from RMST, and an assistant U.S. attorney were in court for a hearing on the application. They were all in support, but Judge Rebecca Beech Smith took four more days before signing off on the order, which prohibited removing any items or making contact with the wreck or even the seafloor around it.

The *Pressure Drop* put into St. John's Harbour in Newfoundland to pick up the Triton team, the Atlantic film crew, and several *Titanic* aficionados. Parks Stephenson, who had been on multiple *Titanic* expeditions with James Cameron, had been invited on the trip for his historical knowledge of the ship. "For me, *Titanic* still has stories to tell, and this is a chance to uncover more of them," he said.

P. H. Nargeolet, Vescovo's technical adviser during the building of the *Limiting Factor* who had been on thirty dives to the wreck, was there for his expertise on both the wreck and the submersible. Microbiologist Lori Johnston, who had left the last metal plate at the wreck to better estimate its rate of decay, was on the trip to supervise placing a new tray on the wreck. Sindbad Rumney-Guggenheim, the great great grandson of Benjamin Guggenheim, a scion of the wealthy American family who perished when the ship sank, was also on board.

As the *Pressure Drop* sailed from St. John's Harbour on a sunny but chilly day in the late afternoon of September 30, everyone gathered in the sky bar, the upper most part of the ship, to take in the views of the colorful wood clapboard houses and the ancient stone battle stations once used to protect the Canadian harbor. The excitement factor was high, and there seemed to be a bit of DiCaprio's enthusiastic Jack

Dawson in everyone. Vescovo had even brought a framed film poster of James Cameron's *Titanic* to hang along with the other sub-themed movie posters decorating the galley. Being slightly superstitious, the crew didn't want to hang it until after the mission was successfully completed.

It would take a day and half to sail the 330 miles to the *Titanic* site, so the first dive was planned for Tuesday morning. Though the schedule called for five dives to film around the entire wreck over eight days, the weather appeared to be conspiring against those plans.

Some 100 miles south of the *Titanic* site, a slow-moving tropical cyclone had become the twelfth named storm and the sixth hurricane of the season. Hurricane Leslie had taken shape on September 22 and meandered around the North Atlantic Ocean. Leslie fell in and out of hurricane status, but regained the distinction on September 28 when it merged with a second frontal system. Projections indicated that Leslie could pass near the *Titanic* site on Friday or Saturday.

The plan was to do as much as possible on the first dive in case the weather was too bad for additional dives. The primary goals were to collect an authorized rusticle, slivers of rust that grew off the iron sides of the *Titanic* from bacterial activity, and also recover and replace a tray placed on the wreck that measured its rate of deterioration.

"We're taking a big roll of the dice because we are a victim of the weather," Vescovo said.

As this was the first extended voyage of the expedition, it would be the longest the team had lived and worked together on the ship. It didn't take long for a rhythm of life on the ship to be established. A morning meeting was set for after breakfast, and then each team went off to prepare for what lay ahead.

On the first afternoon, the entire ship gathered for a ten-minute safety briefing by the first officer. As everyone put their life jackets on, Lahey joked, "Please tell me we have more lifeboats than the *Titanic*."

Everyone ate three meals together. Typically, the ship's crew ate first and fast. For the others, meals became work and social time. The center of most conversations was what could be seen at the *Titanic* wreck.

The quality of the food and the decision to allow alcohol were two critical aspects to the morale of any expedition. Initially, Vescovo was going to hold to the U.S. Navy standards of no alcohol on board, but McCallum, a veteran of long journeys at sea, convinced him otherwise. "You should never go out of sight of land without alcohol," he said. The compromise was

British maritime rules: beer and wine, though the occasional bottle of Crown Royal popped up.

Each afternoon, three large plastic coolers on the upper deck were stocked with wine and beer. Dubbed the sky bar, the area had large, white plastic picnic tables and three stationary deck chairs facing the bow of the ship. After dinner, even in some of the coldest weather, people would drift up to the sky bar to unwind.

The galley was run by chef Manfred Umfahrer, an Austrian who has a friendly round face and a goatee with a point that dangles two inches from his face. Like the other members of the hotel staff, he had lived his life on ships, and didn't seem to mind the long hours and endless days at sea.

Umfahrer rose each day at 4:00 A.M. to begin prepping breakfast. Set meal times were posted. Though breakfast was scheduled for 6:30 A.M., the room was full of crew by 6:15 and empty by 6:45. Lunch was 11:30 A.M. to 12:30 P.M. and dinner from 5:00 to 6:30 P.M.

The ship can carry enough food for up to one and a half months at sea at full capacity of forty-nine. The mess level has a dry storage room with metal shelves containing vats of olives, peppers, and oatmeal. The walk-in refrigerator has large baskets with 100 pieces of fruit in each one. The freezer is stocked with twenty-five pound-roasts and dozens of whole fish, often purchased from local fishermen when the ship ported.

In the mess room, the L-shaped buffet features a cold side and hot side. Above each hot dish is a small, black chalkboard with the name of the dish written in cursive on it. Four entrées are the minimum, six are more like it. In deference to the predominantly Filipino crew, every meal has one or two Asian dishes, such as fried rice or spring rolls.

The one certainty is flavor and spice. Tacos are accompanied by three salsas, hot, hotter, and hottest. Enchiladas are stuffed with chopped jalapeños. Burritos have a kick that makes them taste like authentic Mexican street food.

"The only thing more important than good food is a working coffee machine," McCallum says.

The biggest complaint would become a recurring one: the Wi-Fi was inconsistent and slow when it did work, despite considerable investments to have up to 5 megabits per second download speed ship-wide. The issue was that the bandwidth was divided into groups and when Vescovo was online, more than half of it was automatically allocated to him. Though he had begun to pare down his business commitments in preparation for the deep ocean dives, reducing his load from five to four major companies, he still needed to be in constant contact with his office. But as much as people complained about the poor

Wi-Fi, no one had an issue with the owner taking up so much bandwidth.

"Someone has to pay the bills," McCallum said with a wink.

After dinner on the first night at sea, Geffen prepared a press release to send out after the impending first dive that was cleared by National Geographic.

AT THE SITE OF THE TITANIC WRECK, NORTH ATLANTIC OCEAN—An expedition led by Caladan Oceanic today announces that they have completed the first manned submersible dives to the Titanic wreck in 13 years. Following established U.S. legal protocols, under NOAA's oversight, a team of experts and scientists have been examining the remains of the ship to assess the current condition and project its future. The findings of this expedition will air as a special on the National Geographic Channel and other networks globally in December 2018.

But by the next morning, it began to look like the word "almost" would need to be inserted. When the ship reached the *Titanic* site, the weather was worse than expected. Swells were coming from two directions. Hurricane Leslie was now a massive Category 1 hurricane the size of Connecticut, and though slow moving, it was creeping toward the site from the south at the same time a separate weather front was bearing down from Canada to the north. To complete the trifecta, strong currents were coming across from the European side.

"There's no accurate weather modeling this far out," Captain Buckle explained. "At home the weathermen from town to town can see the weather and report on to the next guy and so forth. In the old days, ships used to wait to feel the swells to know where a storm or hurricane is coming from. Now there are satellite models, but out here they are still best guesses."

The ship was constantly pitching and yawing, left to right, left to right, causing it to feel like you were on an uneven rollercoaster moving in slow motion. Walking required spreading your legs for stability, the "seaman's walk." Sea sickness tablets were a must for all but the most seasoned. On the trip, more than one person would bump their head on the beams inside the staircase, and the occasional glass would slide off a table.

That Tuesday afternoon, a memorial service was held at the site where the *Titanic* sank. With the cameras rolling, McCallum spoke about the tradition of honoring the victims and tossed a wreath overboard. It was the day's only real activity.

By Wednesday morning, the winds were kicking up as high as 43 knots (50 mph), and the ship was rocking badly. There was no realistic chance to attempt a dive. Lahey, Vescovo, McCallum,

Geffen, and Buckle all began discussing what to do. Returning to St. John's and waiting out the storm wasn't an option because of the transit time and the fact that the ship needed to be in New York for the upcoming media day.

Geffen was particularly concerned because the trip was eating up his entire budget for the *Titanic* film, so he was pushing to stay as long as safely possible. If he wasn't able to film at the wreck, he would have to wait another year when the ship headed to the Molloy Deep, as well as having to fund that shoot out of his own pocket. Vescovo wanted to get the footage now, if at all possible, so he didn't have to spend the money to return to the site.

A decision was made to wait one more day, as conditions looked slightly more favorable on Thursday. Buckle had already concluded that Friday was out, because the ship needed time to sail inland in the event Hurricane Leslie continued on its current path.

On Thursday morning, Geffen, McCallum, Lahey, and Buckle were on deck at 6:00 A.M. surveying the conditions. A misty rain was falling, but the sea had calmed slightly and winds were down to 10 knots. They decided to monitor the conditions over the next two hours to determine if a short dive would be prudent.

Lahey and Triton's Magee were against diving. "An eight-hour window is not enough to dive,"

Magee said. "If there was an issue with the sub on the bottom, say it became entrapped in the wreck, it has ninety-six hours of oxygen and we have the assets to go and get it, but not if the ship is blown off the site by a hurricane."

Lahey shook his head. "That would not be a pretty picture."

Still, Geffen was slightly encouraged by the calmer seas. He met with his production team and made final plans to film the dive.

But at 9:00 A.M., the dive was called off by Vescovo. The weather was holding, but it was determined that the window was too narrow and it was just too dangerous.

"The weather is the limiting factor, no pun intended," Lahey said.

Vescovo added, "I feel like the Dallas Cowboys . . . better luck next year."

In a last-ditch effort so as not to have entirely wasted the time and cost of steaming up from Florida and out to the *Titanic* wreck, a revised plan was made. The *Pressure Drop* would sail toward St. John's and the team would attempt an open water dive on Friday closer on the Grand Banks of Newfoundland, a massive underwater plateau off the coast of Canada, where the weather looked to be more favorable. The idea was to practice the launch and recovery of the sub and continue to test its performance.

When the ship arrived at the targeted area, the sea state was elevated to between a 2 and 3, but conditions were far better than at the *Titanic* site. Vescovo, McCallum, Buckle, and Lahey met early Friday morning to discuss whether to dive. Lahey didn't want to risk damaging the sub by attempting to launch and recover in more strenuous conditions than his team had dealt with to date. Buckle felt the dive was doable.

McCallum spoke up, stating the obvious. "We need to show ourselves that we can either do this or we can't," he said. "And if we definitely can't, we might as well pack up and go home because there's no point of heading off to the Southern Ocean."

Lahey shook his head. "There's no fucking way we should dive in this," he said. "It's an unnecessary risk. We'll be diving in Puerto Rico and we can work on the dynamic recovery there."

The Triton crew had never attempted a launch and recovery in conditions bordering on sea state 3. In fact, the toughest seas they had faced were at Advanced Sea Trials, which was just over a sea state 1. Based on the track record to date in the Bahamas, there was little to suggest the dive would be successful in these conditions.

Vescovo listened to all of the voices of the people he would be relying on for guidance over the coming year. He concluded that McCallum was right, they needed to try, because this was the last chance to test themselves in big waters before the potentially violent seas of the Southern Ocean. He had to know if the team could perform.

On the white board that listed the day's plan, McCallum wrote: "Full dress rehearsal for Puerto Rico."

Two hours later, the LARS team readied the *Limiting Factor*. Carrying a pre-dive checklist, Vescovo walked around the sub with Lahey, checking off items one by one. Once they were satisfied, the *Limiting Factor* was attached to the A-frame crane by the main line and moved along the track into position at the back of the aft deck.

Cameras were rolling everywhere. A cameraman was on the *Xeno*. Another camera was filming the deck operations. A drone was flying above, and a diver with a helmet cam was in the water to film the sub from below as it began its descent.

The wild cards were the cameras attached to the sub. Atlantic had rented the cameras from the Woods Hole Oceanographic Institution and contracted for two WHOI personnel to be onboard in the event of problems. The cameras had been delivered to the ship in Newfoundland, leaving no time to test them. Triton had to make significant, if not downright unsightly, modifications to the sub to accommodate the cameras, and it wasn't known if the cameras would affect the sub's electronic functions in the water.

Just before the dive, conditions leveled off, though the swells were still creating white caps. The sky was shrouded in a hazy fog, and a steady wind was blowing. The *Learned Response* support boat that had drawn criticism from Buckle was launched without an issue. The *Xeno*, which would take Vescovo and Lahey to the sub, was next. The *Xeno* circled around to pick them up. As Vescovo was climbing into the *Xeno*, he slipped off of the ladder while transitioning to the boat and fell backward onto the gas tank and bruised a rib. He quickly shook it off.

Kelvin Magee was directing the launch from the bottom deck and Frank Lombardo was operating the A-frame controls. Lombardo, an experienced deck hand with subs, lowered the A-frame as far away from the ship as it would extend, only about five feet. This was the issue that had been identified when the ship was purchased, that the A-frame was not long enough to lower the sub a comfortable distance from the ship. The twelve-ton sub dangled from the A-frame, twisting in the wind.

"Down on the main," Magee said, making a fist and twisting it downward.

Lombardo moved the control arms and slowly lowered the sub. When it was even with the stern, a gust of wind whipped up and slammed the sub into the ship. A loud crunching noise was heard when the sub made contact with the stern.

"Fuck!" Lombardo said, as Magee yelled: "Up on the main! Up on main!"

Lombardo yanked on the up lever, and the sub was lifted above the ship.

A slight crack in the white syntactic foam was visible.

Magee went and inspected it. "Looks cosmetic," Magee shouted. "Let's keep going . . . down on the main . . ."

A visibly frustrated Lombardo lowered the sub again, this time successfully, into the water. Though the sub was just a few feet from the ship, the drag from a sea anchor pulled it away from the stern as the ship was moving through the sea at a slow speed to maintain tension on it. The sub twisted left and right as the crosscurrent hit it.

The *Xeno* approached the sub, but the driver was afraid to get too close for fear of smashing into the cameras mounted on it. This caused Vescovo and Lahey to struggle when grabbing the handrail to climb onto the sub. After several attempts, they managed to board the sub.

Once Vescovo and Lahey were inside the *Limiting Factor* "the swimmer," Steve Chappell, closed the hatch. He then went to work, first removing the railing from the sub and then detaching the towline from the ship. The process took nearly fifteen minutes as the sub tossed like a bucking bronco. When he was finished, he dove into the water and swam to the *Xeno*.

"Are we released?" Vescovo asked the control room.

"Roger that . . ." came the reply.

After final checks and clearance given to dive, the sub slowly disappeared from sight.

The pilots checked in every fifteen minutes, giving their depth and affirming "life support good." Communications during the dive were audible but garbled. Vescovo and Lahey attempted to navigate to the lander dropped earlier but didn't find it. Ninety minutes into the welcome, uneventful dive, the *Limiting Factor* asked for clearance to surface.

For the recovery, Buckle was able to maneuver the ship into a position that blocked the Labrador Current coming down from Canada, the culprit of the choppy seas. This would give the sub more time to pump the water out of the main ballast tanks in the rough conditions. Still, the recovery took far too long for both comfort and safety's sake.

Because of the rough seas, the swimmer Chappell had difficulty attaching the tow line and the sea anchor. Once the sub was in position to be pulled onto the ship, he struggled to clear the water inside of the trunking using the manual pump before he opened the hatch. After ten minutes, he resorted to bath towels. For such a high-tech sub, it was a decidedly low-tech solution that garnered snickers from the onlookers on the ship.

Back on deck, Lahey said, "The sub was about to become a vomitorium."

Multiple problems had occurred inside the sub during the dive. The worst was a small hatch leak. There was enough water ingress that by the end of the ninety-minute dive there was a small puddle of standing water on the bottom of the sub capsule. Though not a safety hazard on a short dive, it would cause a longer dive to be aborted.

The VBT weights jammed on both the starboard and port sides after the first few had released. On all eleven of the sub's dives, the VBT weights had jammed on one side or the other at some point. More work was needed there.

On the electrical front, the pilot's GUI had intermittent failures that caused it to freeze, necessitating rebooting the monitor four times during the dive. The foreground camera used by the pilot for navigation was inoperable.

Even worse than the nonfunctioning foreground camera, one of the exterior cameras provided by WHOI did not work at all, and the other produced substandard footage. Given that Atlantic was looking in the region of $100,000 for the *Titanic* expedition in camera costs for these, Geffen was understandably displeased. He and Syder, his head of production, concluded they would have to look elsewhere for more reliable cameras. However, they were also relieved that the dive hadn't been the lone one to the *Titanic*.

That night after dinner, many of the Triton team gathered in the lounge. Several bottles of red wine and a bottle of Crown Royal were on the table in the middle of the room. They sat around drinking and reviewing the day's events.

"Gentlemen, we got our asses kicked today," Lahey declared. "But we'll get it right."

Sipping a beer in the sky bar, McCallum put a positive spin on the day's events. "We got a real fright, but it was a fright that we needed," he said. "This was the first time we showed we could operate in sea states greater than a meter. We need to break things and make mistakes before we hit harsh conditions. These will be elements on the road to success."

Despite not being able to trumpet a dive to the *Titanic*, the media launch was still on for October 19 in New York. The *Pressure Drop* would sail from Newfoundland to Staten Island. Discovery Channel executives and key media would be invited onboard for a tour and a presentation of the expedition given by the team leaders. The hope was that the media seeing the *Limiting Factor* and footage of it in action would generate some buzz about the Five Deeps Expedition.

Following the media event, the sub needed to be taken back to Triton's new facility in Sebastian, Florida, and completely disassembled to ascertain and fix the cause of the hatch leak, as well as the other items that had failed.

"You have my personal guarantee, we will not see any water in the sphere through the mating ring again," Lahey said to Vescovo.

The following morning, the *Pressure Drop* pulled into St. John's Harbour. Everyone who was not part of the transit crew disembarked. The framed *Titanic* film poster lay unhung on its side leaning against a cabinet in the lounge, a metaphor for the sideways journey that this leg of the expedition had become.

CHAPTER 10
WEATHERING STORMS BIG AND SMALL

Time was running short for Captain Stuart Buckle to leave port in Newfoundland to arrive in New York in time for the planned media launch of the Five Deeps Expedition. Hurricane Leslie, which had knocked the *Pressure Drop* off the *Titanic* site, was still churning in the North Atlantic, just above Newfoundland. Compounding the problem were the remnants of Hurricane Michael, which had come up the east coast of the U.S., skirted Nova Scotia and Newfoundland, and was finally heading out into the open waters.

Buckle waited until the worst of Hurricane Michael had passed. On October 14, with winds still gusting to 68 knots and a twenty-foot sea swell, Buckle decided that conditions were safe enough to sail for New York, giving him four days to make the October 19 event. The captain of a 180-meter ship holed up in St. John's Harbour radioed and called him a "crazy little guy" for sailing in such conditions.

As the *Pressure Drop* hit the open waters, high winds and sea swells slowed the ship from its average of 9–10 knots to 6–7 knots, pushing the estimated arrival time from midday on the 18th to the morning of the 19th, the day of the event. The following morning, it became clear that the ship would not make it in time for the afternoon event.

Geffen discussed the situation with Discovery Channel executives and they decided to proceed and hold the event in a conference room at its midtown offices. The fact that the launch would be missing its star—the submersible—added to the existing tension among the principals. In the two weeks preceding the event, an email skirmish had broken out over the media launch and who could do what regarding press.

Though Atlantic Productions had contractual control on behalf of Discovery over the expedition's media as part of its deal with Vescovo, Triton was pushing back in an effort to protect its marketing interests. Both Bruce Jones and Lahey claimed they were not bound by Vescovo's contract with Atlantic as they weren't party to it, and so they had scheduled their own event aboard the ship. They held the exclusive rights until February 1 to sell the ship and the sub, and they felt they needed their own press coverage to reach interested buyers.

Geffen was among the best producers in the nonfiction film world at promoting his projects, but he told Vescovo that Discovery was insisting on holding back the release of more information to generate the maximum amount of buzz all at once. He also had considerable experience with multilayered projects. Discovery's position, he explained to Vescovo, was that Triton should invite its media list to the main event, and not do anything separate in an uncoordinated manner.

But while Caladan and Atlantic had agreed that the media strategy would be jointly coordinated, Triton felt this was limiting their ability to market the sub.

A compromise was reached allowing Triton to hold a smaller event on the ship with industry press. However, when it was evident that the ship would not make it to New York, Triton canceled its event and invited their press contacts to the Discovery event.

The day before the media launch, the team leaders all attended a small event at the Explorers Club. Vescovo had recently become a member of the Explorers Club and had completed its "Grand Slam," summiting the highest peaks on each of the seven continents and skiing at least 100 kilometers at the North and South poles. With the planned deep dives, he was now taking things to a whole new level. At the club, he was presented with a flag to take with him in the sub to the bottom of the five oceans. When the expedition was complete, the flag would take its place among the others hanging in the club, including one from the first Moon landing.

That night, the group gathered for dinner at Sip Sak, a Turkish restaurant in midtown Manhattan. Lahey, Jamieson, McCallum, and P. H. Nargeolet were all there. Vescovo arrived a half hour late, after doing a radio interview that ran over. Geffen had other plans and did not attend the dinner.

After a spirited dinner, Vescovo invited everyone to see his apartment in Trump World Tower by the United Nations. On the walk over, Lahey quipped to McCallum, "Will the Donald be there?" Someone who overheard the comment pointed out that it was the first mention of Trump he had heard in all the hours the team leaders had been together.

The mood was light, thanks to heavy pours of Turkish wine from the restaurant's extremely friendly proprietor. The group rode the elevators to the 76th-floor apartment, which has one of those signature New York high-rise vistas in which the building lights seem to stretch forever. The apartment was decorated with touches of Vescovo's love of exploring, and the refrigerator, as he self-depreciatingly pointed out, was filled only with cans of Diet Coke, his daily fuel.

As a social evening away from the ship, it went well. There was a feeling of unity and that everyone was in this together. As Lahey summed it up, "Pretty fuckin' fun night."

• • •

The following day was a contrast in possibility and reality. The expedition team gathered in a conference room at Discovery's offices to announce a five-part series on the Five Deeps Expedition and to discuss deep ocean exploration. The first press had appeared that morning, a small piece in the TV section of the *New York Post*, an exclusive given to the paper. The expedition's website—fivedeeps.com—had just gone live.

Discovery had invited several press outlets to the event, including the BBC, Reuters, the Associated Press, and CNN. The Richards Group, a Dallas-based PR and marketing firm that Vescovo had hired to represent him, invited the *Wall Street Journal*'s science editor, a *Forbes* writer, three producers for CBS's *Sunday Morning*, and an *ABC World News* correspondent. However, because the sub didn't make it, none of the high-end organizations attended.

But the show went on anyway. Geffen moderated a panel discussion with Vescovo, Lahey, Ramsay, Jamieson, and McCallum, and showed clips of the sub diving. There was no shortage of platitudes and hype.

Geffen opened by talking about Atlantic's 25-year working relationship with Discovery. "We've done some pretty big things, but I think they realize this could top most of them to follow this expedition," he said.

Lahey called the sub "the equivalent of a moonshot." Geffen introduced Ramsay, the designer, as "the new Jony Ive," a reference to the legendary head of product design at Apple, and he referred to McCallum as a "mastermind" in planning. McCallum declared that the sub was "the most significant exploration vehicle since Apollo 11." Vescovo was always embarrassed by those who made this—to him—very hyperbolic comparison. On the science side, Jamieson talked about how the ocean could only be fully understood by studying its depths, a door that the *Limiting Factor* was now set to open, adding, "this could be a groundbreaking expedition in terms of understanding the Hadal Zone."

However, at one point, there was an awkward exchange. When Geffen was talking about diving to 2,000 meters in one of Ray Dalio's subs that had been built by Triton, Ramsay perked up. "I do hope you didn't take one of our other subs to 2,000 meters because it's 1,000-meter rated," Ramsay said.

"We definitely went to at least 1,600 meters," Geffen countered.

Lahey stepped into the breach. "You wouldn't have gone below 1,000 meters," he said. "It could be 1,600 feet."

"No . . . it was 1,600 meters," Geffen said, before changing the subject.

At the end, McCallum summed up the expedition in his irreverent manner. "We're taking a group of people who haven't worked together before and we are sending them off on a mission that has never been done before in a piece of machinery that has never operated before," he said. "What could possibly go wrong?"

As everyone on the dais knew, plenty could and already had gone wrong. The reality of the situation was slightly different than the optimism filling the presentation. At present, instead of being docked in Staten Island for media tours, the *Pressure Drop* was fifty miles off the coast of Virginia, caked with salt from the battering it took dodging two hurricanes, carrying a crew that was exhausted from the ordeal. The ship was in the process of transporting the star of the series, the *Limiting Factor*, back to Triton's facility in Florida for refit.

Because there was no sub to see, the resulting press coverage was tepid. There were no TV cameras at the event. The BBC and Sky News did features on the expedition after conducting one-on-one interviews with Vescovo and Lahey. One science reporter from Reuters bizarrely asked Vescovo in an interview how he would get in and out of the sub—at the bottom of the ocean. Vescovo politely explained how that would not be possible. *Forbes* posted a story online based on information it was provided, as its reporter did not attend. However, the story contained multiple inaccuracies—it even misstated the name of the sub—and accusations began flying back and forth over who was responsible.

The biggest problem with the *Forbes* story was a quote attributed to Geffen, which Geffen said did not come from him. He was quoted saying that the ocean "can be used for medical innovations such as finding cures for Alzheimer's." Since 2010, researchers had been studying whether the sea squirt, human's closest invertebrate relative, could aid in Alzheimer's drug development by testing whether the accumulation of plaques and tangles that mar the brain could be undone in sea squirts. But this was far beyond the scope of any science the expedition was contemplating and, in fact, could create regulatory problems with countries whose shores bordered the oceans.

Jamieson explained that merely saying the expedition was looking for pharmaceuticals or cures for cancers or Alzheimer's could endanger their permits. The reason was that anything in a country's Exclusive Economic Zone (EEZ), the area stretching 200 nautical miles from its shore, is the property of that nation under the 1982 United Nations Convention on the Law of the Sea.

"We cannot simply go into someone else's EEZ

232

and go looking for potential pharma, without permission," the scientist emailed Vescovo. "That is THEFT. I led the expedition 'PharmaDEEP' to Antarctica in 2015, where we did have permits, and 6 months later I was nearly ARRESTED for breaking the agreement as the person who had clearance to allow screening for pharma and passed the sample on to someone who had not. I didn't even know. In the event of 'illegal' prospecting it is the COLLECTOR who goes to prison, and in PharmaDEEP and indeed the 5-deeps, that is me. I ain't going to jail on this one!"

Vescovo's position was unequivocal: the expedition needed to make sure it was clear to the press that there was no biomedical prospecting occurring. If there was any possibility of the dive permits being jeopardized, Vescovo said that he would pull the science mission from the expedition from that leg, or *in toto*, to ensure the permits needed to dive remained in place. To prevent a potential conflict, there needed to be better—and accurate—communication with the media.

For his part, McCallum thought the New York event was a poorly produced waste of time. He wrote Vescovo an email calling the media day "amateur night" and criticized Geffen for grandstanding about past Atlantic films, for speaking with cue cards and for the quote in

Forbes. He concluded that the "riff-raff media will always get it a bit wrong, but *Forbes* is a pretty good player so I think they were given the wrong info."

For his part, Geffen pointed out that a Discovery executive was supposed to be the MC for the event, but Geffen had to step in last minute. And of course, the media event had been planned around the sub being there—and when it wasn't, then obviously the event was less exciting and drew fewer journalists.

In the rush of responding to the over 100 emails a day he was fielding, Vescovo accidentally emailed McCallum's critique to Geffen as part of a forwarded email chain about correcting the *Forbes* story.

"Anthony was upset and called me," Vescovo said. "He said, 'Rob is unprofessional, but I will work with him.' For all Rob's gripes about Anthony, Anthony has equal gripes about Rob and the way he handles the expedition."

Vescovo was frustrated at the tense relationship that was developing between the two strong personalities before the expedition had even gotten underway. He himself was not particularly pleased with certain aspects of the media coverage thus far, but also didn't think McCallum appreciated that Geffen had delivered a five-part Discovery Channel series and a multi-broadcast coproduction (including National Geographic

Channel) on the *Titanic*. "These are no mean feats that I don't think Rob fully appreciates," he said. "I do, anyway."

Geffen told Vescovo that he did not speak directly to the *Forbes* reporter and that she had taken the quotation out of context from press materials that Discovery sent out, as one of the scientists who planned to join the expedition in the Southern Ocean had done research in that area. As for the debate over the depth he dived in Dalio's Triton sub, Geffen brushed it off as "banter by a Brit confusing meters and feet."

For whatever reason, perhaps because of all the back and forth or in spite of it, the *Forbes* story was never corrected.

Small skirmishes like this one were causing Vescovo to become increasingly frustrated with the overall state of affairs. For all that had gone wrong in private, announcing the Five Deeps Expedition publicly would mean that any future failures would be out in the open—widely so. For starters, it wasn't clear when—or even if—the first dive would actually come off.

The *Limiting Factor*, which had only been partially functioning as it should, was being completely disassembled for repairs, and the *Pressure Drop* was headed to dry dock to be outfitted with a massive new sonar. These events needed to come to a successful conclusion before the Puerto Rico Trench dive could happen in mid-December, or the dive would have to be postponed so that expedition could make the mid-January weather window in the Southern Ocean.

"At the end of the day, it was Rob's recommendation to try for *Titanic*, as well as saying we could make New York," Vescovo said. "I know, it was weather that held us up, but at the end of the day, we didn't deliver, and we had a poor schedule to make both happen. He didn't put enough safety margin in, and I ended up wasting maybe $300,000, at least, steaming up to St. John's and now back down on a failed mission. And again, I know he would scream 'weather! hurricanes!' but even those need to be factored into planning and if we have any major issues on the PR Trench, I'm going to have to start asking hard questions of Rob as well as Triton on why we keep failing in missions."

McCallum took it all in stride. "That's why I had a name tag printed for myself with 'Scapegoat' on it," he said. "My job is to take the criticism and make things work."

The *Pressure Drop* arrived in Fort Pierce, Florida, on October 25 and offloaded the *Limiting Factor* for its refit at Triton's new, larger facility in nearby Sebastian. The ship then headed for dry dock in Curaçao, off the coast of Venezuela, where it would be outfitted with the sonar. Because of the tight schedule, the *Limiting*

Factor would need to be transported to Puerto Rico to rejoin the ship there for the first planned deep dive to the Puerto Rico Trench, the deepest part of the Atlantic Ocean. The situation was less than optimal, and a bit risky, but it was the only way to fix the sub and install the sonar at the same time.

The day the sub arrived, Triton sent an estimate of costs to Dick DeShazo for the maintenance, totaling $146,846. This included fixing the sphere leak, the VBT weight system, the air conditioning system, the trunk pump, as well as multiple electronic issues. "I gulped when I saw it," DeShazo said.

DeShazo forwarded the estimate to Vescovo, who was understandably miffed. He felt that many of the items were design flaws and therefore should be covered as warranty items, and he asked DeShazo to detail them. Still, he said that he was okay funding the estimate "for the sake of domestic peace," though he wanted the warranty items "where there is clear poor workmanship or a screw-up by Triton" applied to Triton's side of the ledger in the onward sale agreement.

"They have gotten into the awful habit of just throwing rather large costs, willy-nilly, into a bucket that charged Caladan and expecting me to pay 100 percent, on time, with no explanations, cost backup, or pushback," Vescovo said. "It's getting out of hand and as a financially challenged organization, they need to do things far better when it comes to cost estimating, taking responsibility for their errors, and billing properly, not to mention being far more sensitive to cost overruns and managing costs."

Sub designer John Ramsay quickly diagnosed the biggest problem, the leak, and came up with a fix. He found that the leaking in the pressure hull was the result of the opposing halves of the main pressure hull sliding, ever so slightly relative to each other against the equatorial ring plate around them, whenever the sub was lifted by crane. This was being caused by movement in the frame attached to the hull that held the syntactic foam. His solution, which he cleared with certifier DNV-GL, was to install what he called a Circumferential Preload System. This basically entailed placing a tight metal band around the hull at an angle to prevent the two halves from shifting.

"I knew right away what the issue was, but it took a while to come up with a sure-thing fix," Ramsay said. "I'm pretty sure it won't be leaking anymore."

While the *Limiting Factor* was undergoing its repairs, the *Pressure Drop* headed for the Damen shipyard in Curaçao. Once out of the water, a gondola on the keel would be installed, followed by the massive sonar. Damen was also contracted to build out a new davit, the small crane used to lower the *Learned Response* support boat, as a solution to replacing the boat altogether.

Released in 2018, the EM 124 sonar was the fifth generation of a range of new multibeam systems from Kongsberg Maritime, a Norwegian company. It is the most advanced civilian multibeam sonar echo sounder available and could generate high-resolution seabed images for mapping from shallow waters to full ocean depths with quite wide "swath" coverage and resolution. The sonar would allow the expedition to map the ocean trenches and to determine with great accuracy the true depths of the oceans. This was the first one Kongsberg had sold; thus, it carried the serial number 001.

But before the installation of the gondola and sonar even began, there were two major vendor failures and a price increase to boot. Forty-eight hours after DeShazo accepted Damen's bid on the advice of Thome Croatia, the company hired by Vescovo's Caladan to oversee the ship's operations, and wired $100,000 to start the project, Damen advised him of a 15 percent jump in price over the agreed-upon quote. Next, Damen notified him that there would be a delay of several weeks, as it had ordered the wrong type of steel for the gondola.

Then, Kongsberg literally misplaced its $1 million sonar during the shipping process.

The sonar was to be loaded onto a cargo ship in Norway. The Kongsberg team in Curaçao waiting for the sonar tracked the ship and its arrival—but it turned out that the sonar had not been loaded on the ship and was still in Norway. Kongsberg scrambled to send the sonar by air freight and agreed to eat the $50,000 shipping cost.

While all this was being sorted out, the *Pressure Drop* was killing time off the coast of Haiti waiting for word on when to port. "I think the authorities were a little suspicious of us and what we were doing," Buckle said. "I was glad to get word to port."

Pulling the contract from Damen was not a viable option so the price increase was reluctantly agreed to—it was still a "fair" price in Vescovo's view, who had actually worked in a shipyard at one point in his career. As a practical measure, the expedition could not afford the time to find another shipyard and still have a realistic shot at making the Southern Ocean weather window.

The ensuing weeks were disorderly. Thome had a representative on-site, but he had little success pushing Damen to move faster. Vescovo ended up hiring Brian Gamet, a sonar expert from Geosight Land & Hydrographic Surveys, to serve as the owner's rep and supervise the installation of the sonar package.

McCallum, who had initially recommended the shipyard, was caught in a tough spot. He was both pushing the Curacao shipyard to speed up the job, while simultaneously threatening to take up the matter of the inflated costs and delays with the higher-ups at Damen headquarters.

Midway through the process, Damen replaced its shipyard manager with a more experienced and responsive one, and things started to improve. Still, what was supposed to be a two-week job was turning into a six-week one. Things were not under control, and Damen was not responding as Vescovo knew they should, or could.

On November 23, an increasingly frustrated Vescovo summarily dropped what he was doing and flew in his jet with his copilot all the way to Curaçao. He and Buckle demanded a meeting with the new shipyard manager, which they were granted. The executive sheepishly admitted to a series of start-up errors and promised to accelerate the project without sacrificing quality. Vescovo was warily satisfied with the meeting and asked Buckle to maintain a close eye on the work.

With Buckle keeping close tabs, the sonar installation was finished and the ship was refloated on December 8. That afternoon, the Damen shipyard operations manager handed Buckle an invoice for $981,000, bringing the dockyard total costs to over $1.1 million, or roughly double the amount of what had been agreed to in a fixed-price contract. It had become apparent that Damen had underbid the contract to secure it, and then racked up time and materials costs, and were now threatening to hold the ship hostage until the bill was paid. This was, unfortunately, a routine occurrence in what Vescovo called "the unscrupulous world of ship repair."

Vescovo was in a no-win position in the short term. The contract carried a dispute resolution mechanism: arbitration in Rotterdam. Matt Lipton, Vescovo's attorney, found an attorney there in the event that an arbitration over costs, or the threat of one, became necessary. However, that didn't solve the current dilemma of getting the ship released.

McCallum contacted the shipyard's managing director, Lodewijk Franken, and insisted that Damen release the ship for the agreed-upon amount in the fixed price contract. "We expect Damen to honour that contract in its entirety," he emailed. "The Damen name is riding on that outcome."

Franken responded that he did not want to enter arbitration and suggested the parties settle the matter "around the table" after he prepared a justification for additional charges. He conceded that some of the charges were incorrect, and agreed to allow the ship to sail if Buckle signed a completion certificate and Caladan paid 85 percent of the previously agreed-upon amount. DeShazo promptly wired $200,000 so the ship could sail for Puerto Rico, which it did on December 10 with an ETA of December 13, to a massive collective sigh of relief from everyone on the expedition team.

It turned out that the fixed price contract was full of holes and had not been properly vetted by the ship's management firm, Thome, whom Vescovo and Lipton had relied on to ensure it was a fair contract *without* holes. DeShazo had signed the contract and wired the deposit while riding in a taxi to the media launch event. He had done so relying on the advice of Roko Stanic, the senior manager at Thome Croatia. However, it turned out that Stanic and McCallum, who had recommended Damen, had just passed along the contract without conducting any due diligence on the Curaçao yard or performing a thorough review of the contract.

"Ultimate responsibility lies with me, and I should have noticed the lackadaisical attitude of Thome, the lower level of involvement of Rob, and trusting Dick to make sure the contract was complete," Vescovo said. "It is turning out, to my surprise, that I have a lot more general business experience than the other members of the team and I should have taken more direct control over this contract. But Jesus, I can't do everything or be everywhere, and I am paying a lot of money to people . . . to handle these details, but unfortunately, people sometimes just don't execute. They like to say they are, and tout their maritime experience, like Rob or Bruce Jones did, but when it comes to results, people just too often can fall short. I trusted the so-called experts, and got lightly burned. And good Lord, if we hadn't gone all hands on deck, and if Stu Buckle, who is just extraordinary, hadn't been there and stepped up, we would have been there another month."

DeShazo prepared a minutely detailed, 21-page charge-rebuttal memo outlining Caladan's position on every single billable item and challenging certain overages and many of the change orders. He then subtracted the $304,541 that he was disputing, and paid the remainder of the bill, bringing the total outlay to $686,560, far less than $1.081 million billed. Vescovo swore he would go to war with them, on principle, if they challenged even a single line item of their rebuttal. He never had to—Damen never responded.

As the work continued on the *Limiting Factor*, Vescovo, Lahey, and DeShazo explored options for safely transporting the *Limiting Factor* to Puerto Rico to rejoin the *Pressure Drop*. The three options were to ship the *LF* in its special standard container to Puerto Rico for pickup, to hire a dedicated ship to move it from Florida and do an at-sea transfer, or to find a "friend of Triton," such as Ray Dalio's ship the *Alucia*, to transport it in exchange for a dive or some other consideration.

"I feel like I have to micro-manage Triton on the *LF* shipping," Vescovo said. "I don't trust them 100 percent on this. They can be far, far too over-confident on things they don't do regularly—or even regularly—and as an organization are just overly optimistic a lot of the time. But this transport was a huge deal, and I wasn't sure they fully appreciated the stakes."

In addition to damage or loss, there were concerns with customs in Puerto Rico even though it is a U.S. territory. "The last thing we want is the *LF* sitting in a debarkation area under lock and key, waiting for paperwork or a bureaucratic snafu, or god forbid, the container being sent to the wrong port," Vescovo told DeShazo.

The dedicated ship option priced out between $100,000 and $140,000, money that could be better spent elsewhere assuming a reliable cargo company could even be engaged. Lahey estimated the third option could be in the same neighborhood, as any ship would have to relocate. The decision was somewhat reluctantly made to ship the sub on a TOTE Maritime cargo ship, at a far more reasonable cost of $25,200.

On December 5, the *Limiting Factor* was

loaded onto a 40-foot, flat rack truck and secured with six lashings rated to 5,000 kilograms (11,000 pounds) each for the trip from Triton's facility to the port in Jacksonville. Kelvin Magee and a colleague followed the truck and then supervised the loading of the sub onto the cargo ship. "We had a lot of strange looks from other drivers," Magee said.

"This transport of the *LF* scares the bejeezus out of me," Vescovo said. "I have nightmares of the container getting lost, on fire, or falling overseas during the transit. I keep recalling that Jim Cameron's *Deepsea Challenger* caught on fire while it was being transported."

On December 10, right on schedule, the TOTE Maritime cargo ship carrying the *Limiting Factor* arrived in Puerto Rico and was cleared for entry by Departamento de Hacienda de Puerto Rico, the nation's Department of Treasury. Lahey and, at Vescovo's insistence, DeShazo were at the port to meet the ship and supervise the offload of the sub into a secure storage facility.

As relieved as Vescovo was to have the crown jewel of the expedition safe, he was becoming increasingly concerned with the mistakes and missteps that had piled up before the first deep dive had been attempted. The delays had also caused the dedicated science week that Vescovo had promised Jamieson to be scrapped. Any science done in the Puerto Rico Trench would have to be lumped in with the ocean floor mapping and the dive days.

"We have a long way to go to execute this mission, and so far, a lot of things haven't gone right," he said. "We can rack them up to weather, human error, bad luck, but I am getting very concerned because too many things seem to not be going our way, too often."

He, like everyone involved, hoped to soon turn the corner, starting with a successful dive to the deepest point in the Atlantic Ocean.

CHAPTER 11
OFF THE DEEP END

The Five Deeps expedition felt like it was at the crossroads. The *Limiting Factor* was heading into its first deep ocean dive, the Puerto Rico Trench in the Atlantic Ocean, but no one was sure if they would be able to achieve the goal. They hoped they could. They thought they could. Certainly, after three years of planning, two sea trials, and an open water dive in the North Atlantic, they should have been sure. But based on their rocky track record and series of engineering setbacks, they weren't sure they actually could.

On December 12, the night before the *Pressure Drop* ported in San Juan, the Triton team gathered for dinner at an Italian restaurant in their hotel and discussed whether the sub was ready. Most agreed that it was, but there was some hesitation, as it had not been back in the water after spending six weeks in the shop, during which time it had been disassembled.

"Man, I fuckin' hope we get this right," Lahey said, sipping red wine. "No, we *will* get this right."

The *Pressure Drop* came alongside at Puerto

Nuevo Terminal in the industrial area of San Juan Harbor the following morning at 6:00 A.M. The ground crew went to work loading the *Limiting Factor* onto the ship so that it could sail that afternoon. For all the anxiety over having to ship the sub to Puerto Rico to rejoin the *Pressure Drop* after it went to dry dock, the process went smoothly.

However, on the run from Curaçao, Captain Buckle and his first engineer had noticed that the ship's starboard propeller was operating at only 65 percent capacity. Yet, despite the compromised prop and the installation of the bulky gondola and sonar, Buckle calculated that the ship's average speed had actually *increased* since it left dry dock. One factor was the cleaning of the barnacles from the hull. The other was that the gondola had lowered the hull slightly in the water and also unexpectedly produced a sort of Venturi effect which had reduced the overall drag of the ship.

A diver was hired to check the prop while the ship was in port in San Juan, but there was no visual evidence of what was causing the prop to give off the unusual resonance which had reduced its operating speed. The repair would have to be done later, at some point before the ship set out to cross the Southern Ocean in early January. For now, the focus was the first deep ocean dive.

The *Pressure Drop* sailed at 6:00 P.M. on the

13th. Everyone gathered in the sky bar to take in the view of El Morro Castle as the ship departed the harbor. Absent was Geffen, the series executive producer, who was busy with other obligations.

At an all-hands meeting, McCallum reviewed the dive program. The schedule allowed for four days of diving. These were to include a test dive with Vescovo and Lahey, a certification dive with Lahey and DNV-GL's Struwe, Vescovo's solo dive to the bottom, and a science dive. Jamieson wasn't happy with the setup, as he had originally been promised a week of dives, but there was little he could do about it.

Lahey presented Vescovo with a desktop model of the *Limiting Factor* for his office. Vescovo thanked him. He held up the model and cracked a smile.

"It's a little damaged," he said, pointing to a nick in the side.

"So is the real *LF*," Lahey retorted, prompting chuckles all around the room.

The first thirty-six hours were taken up mapping the Puerto Rico Trench with data collected by the newly installed Kongsberg EM 124 multibeam echo sounder to identify the deepest point. Created by the shifting of the North American and Caribbean tectonic plates, the subduction zone is situated on the boundary of the Caribbean

Sea and the Atlantic Ocean, roughly 500 miles off the coast. It was discovered in 1876 by Great Britain's HMS *Challenger*. The trench's deepest point had been identified, but not verified by physical visitation, in 1939 by an echo sounder on the USS *Milwaukee*, hence it had been named the Milwaukee Deep. The most recent manned dive to the deeper depths of the trench had been done in 1964 by the French submersible *Archimède*, but it was a science mission and was not focused on verifying the deepest point. Based on the early data and more recently published surveys done using remote operating vehicles, both Jamieson and geologist Heather Stewart posited that there was, in fact, a deeper and unvisited point to the east of the Milwaukee Deep.

Cassie Bongiovanni, a hydrographer, had been hired as the expedition's lead mapper. For the native Texan, it was something of a dream job, as she had recently completed her master's degree in Ocean Mapping at the University of New Hampshire's School of Marine Science and Ocean Engineering. Though only in her mid-twenties, she had worked with NOAA's mapping efforts in the agency's Integrated Ocean and Coastal Mapping (IOCM) department after Hurricane Sandy, worked with autonomous mapping vehicles in the Antarctic, and helped map seeps off the west coast of the U.S. Bongiovanni would be on board to produce the first detailed 3D maps of all the trenches visited by the expedition.

Stewart would review the new maps and compare them to existing images. In addition to finding the deepest point, the goal was to collect more data on the area in the form of high-resolution images for further study of the trench. Ideally, the sub would also be able to collect rock samples using the manipulator arm and place them in the landers' baskets.

A massive earthquake in the trench in 1918 had caused a destructive tsunami and chances were that another would happen again in our lifetimes. "We just don't have much data on the trench, so predicting when and if there will be another tsunami is guesswork," Stewart said. "We're hoping to begin to advance that study with the mapping, image capturing, and samples."

The first dive was set for December 15 at 8:30 A.M. As the Triton team ran through its prelaunch checklist of the *Limiting Factor*, the Atlantic team readied its cameras. Four were mounted inside the sub. One cameraman would be on the ship, one in the *Xeno*, and one operating a drone. The four new underwater cameras capable of capturing high-definition images, two on the sub and one on each lander, had come from Deepsea Power & Light, a Triton vendor.

"Our challenge is that on the underwater

cameras, none of the footage just plays easily, and none of the footage works in our editing system straightaway," Atlantic's Ian Syder explained. "So to convert it all and make it viewable, we have built an edit system on board. The footage also requires real-time conversion."

Despite the fact that the Triton team had been working on the sub for more than a month and a half, six hours after the scheduled time the sub was still not ready to launch. Lahey was at wits' end as small problems reared themselves, ranging from electronics that wouldn't start up to the levers operating the A-frame crane needing WD-40.

"That's what fucking happens with these subs," Lahey said, as he barreled across the deck to troubleshoot yet another niggling issue.

Finally, at 3:00 P.M., Lahey and Vescovo climbed into the *Limiting Factor* for a dive to 1,000 meters to test its systems. The sub didn't make it past 100 meters. On its descent, water began leaking in, noticeably, through the finely machined hatch. The situation wasn't life-threatening, but it wasn't diveable either.

The science team, which had risen at 6:00 A.M., was more successful with its lander deployments. The landers recovered tubes full of arthropods and a hagfish, a slimy sea creature that has no skull and breathes through its anus. A camera on one of the landers captured a two-foot-long shark with beady eyes attempting to dine on the hagfish, only to have the hagfish eject slime into the shark's mouth and scare it away. People took turns gathering around Jamieson's computer and watching.

That evening, as the sunset over the nearby uninhabited Desecheo Island produced a sweeping rainbow, the Triton team went to work fixing the leak. Magee shaved ¼ millimeter off the "O ring" housing around the hatch to get a better seal. He then boarded the sub on the deck. Lahey closed the hatch and filled the trunking with tap water. There was no leakage. Lahey was convinced they had fixed the issue and that the sub was ready to go.

But the following day, the 16th, several issues again delayed the launch, creating frustration all around. A panel covering cables running from the outside of the sub through penetrator plates to the inside was missing, apparently lost at sea during the previous day's abbreviated dive. Magee tied the wires together to secure them. "Panel's just cosmetic," he said.

On the electronics front, Blades had his hands full. The forward camera on the sub was not working, and there was no GPS signal. Two of the landers were also out of service because of modem issues.

When Vescovo indicated to Lahey that Blades needed to fix the landers since they were needed for navigation on the bottom, Lahey curtly said, "Tom is focused on the comms for the dive, and we'll address the landers afterward." Blades chimed in, "I'm absolutely sure I can fix it, just not in the next half hour."

The dive with Lahey piloting and Vescovo riding shotgun finally got underway at 3:15 P.M. It was aborted five minutes later because the hatch was leaking slightly—yet again.

Though the launch had gone fairly well, the recovery was messy. Because the *Limiting Factor* surfaced so quickly, the ship had to reposition itself. While this was occurring, the sub was left pitching from side to side in the choppy water for over thirty minutes. Then, after the swimmer, Colin Quigley, had attached the main line and the two side tag lines to the ship's crane, one of the tag lines snapped. Without both tag lines, the deck crew would have no way to fully stabilize the sub when it was raised out of the water by the A-frame crane.

Frank Lombardo, one of Triton's deck hands and maintenance techs who has a "failure will not happen on my watch" attitude, radioed for the *Learned Response* to pick him up. The tender zipped back to the ship. Wearing no life jacket, he jumped into the support boat and rushed out to the sub grasping a new tagline. Without hesitation, the Floridian and expert diver dove in the water and clipped the tagline to the sub. He then swam back to the support boat.

The recovery process took more than an hour, during which time Vescovo—for the first time in his life caused by rough seas—lost his lunch.

When the sub was finally in position behind the ship, Vescovo climbed out of the hatch and grabbed the side railing attached to it for entrances and exits. Just as he steadied himself to step into the tender, a white-capped wave struck the sub, and he was tossed into the water. Quigley, who had already broken a rib the day before, dived in after him, as Vescovo swam to the tender and climbed in.

Minutes later, Vescovo was back on board the *Pressure Drop*. His fireproof pilot suit was soaking wet. Typically, after each dive he would give a brief on-camera interview to the Atlantic film crew, but this time he brushed by them without saying anything. He walked through the control room with barely a pause and down the hallway. As he made a turn into the stairway to go to his cabin, he left behind wet footprints and a trail of disappointment with everyone involved.

As he entered his cabin, one of the stewards was restocking his supply of Diet Coke. The steward took one look at the dripping wet Vescovo and asked, "Are you okay?"

Vescovo managed a smile. "I've had better days."

Meanwhile, with Lahey now back on deck, the

Triton crew was struggling to maneuver the sub in the right position to lift it out of the water. It was bobbing around just inches from the stern as Magee tried to tighten the tag lines and stabilize it before hoisting it onto the ship. After a few harrowing moments, they succeeded.

Once the sub was on deck and locked in place, Lahey yelled, "Nice fuckin' job Magee!" Lahey, Magee, and the two crane operators hugged. As poorly as the entire day had gone, disaster had been averted and the *Limiting Factor* was safely back in its cradle.

The atmosphere at dinner was surprisingly light. Lahey sat with Vescovo, and the two discussed the leaky hatch and a problem with the main ballast tanks that needed to be corrected. Lahey, who was still inside the sub when Vescovo fell into the ocean, joked that when he saw Vescovo soaking wet, he thought that he had gone for a swim because it was such a beautiful day. "Well, the water was warm," Vescovo said.

As he left the table, Lahey turned serious and threw some of his typical optimism on the problems. "We're gonna get it right, do it again tomorrow and get the trench done."

"That's all I want for Christmas," Vescovo said.

On Monday, December 17th, Lahey and Vescovo boarded the sub for a third test dive. This one really needed to be successful, as there was only one more diving day left on the schedule for Vescovo to attempt his solo dive.

The *Pressure Drop* had moved to the leeward side of the island, where the seas were calmer. Though the launch was uneventful, the hatch began to leak as the sub descended. This time it was more like seepage than a trickle of water, so Lahey and Vescovo decided to continue the dive.

When they reached the bottom, at 1,000 meters (3,280 feet), they radioed that they were going to look for the lander. Kelvin Magee, who was serving as the comms officer, smiled. "Small victories," he said to the anxious room. "We need some."

Inside the sub, Vescovo was piloting and things were going well. The water ingress from the hatch had stopped as the water pressure had evidently sealed the hatch. He and Lahey were marveling at the exotic sea creatures they could see through the viewports. This was what a dive was supposed to be like.

"Should I try the manipulator arm?" Vescovo asked.

"That's up to you," Lahey replied.

"I just want to see if we can get it out," Vescovo said.

"We can definitely get it out," Lahey said.

Vescovo powered up the hydraulic system, the manipulator controls, and then grasped the arm's control lever and extended the arm. Lahey was pressed against the viewport, watching intently. As the massive hydraulic arm with a claw on the end came into view and extended away from the sub, Lahey said, "There's your arm." As Lahey turned away and prepared to make a call to the surface, Vescovo maneuvered the arm for a few seconds and began to re-cradle it for ascent.

Suddenly, there was a snapping noise, followed by a small puff of sea dust coming off the seafloor.

"What the hell was that?" Lahey said.

"We just lost the arm," Vescovo said.

Lahey's eyes widened. "No . . ."

Without saying a word, Vescovo pointed for him to look outside his portal and see the detached arm. "Oh my God . . ." Lahey lamented.

Vescovo stowed the arm's control lever and leaned back in his seat, utterly deflated. "I don't know where we go from here, Patrick."

Without the significant weight of the manipulator arm, the sub began an unplanned ascent.

"Surface, we just lost the manipulator arm," Vescovo radioed. "We are on our way up."

As Vescovo's voice filled the control room, some people put their heads in their hands, others' eyes widened in disbelief. One person choked on his soda. No one said anything.

Magee, who was not expecting a comms check for another few minutes, picked up the handheld microphone. "Roger that," he said in an even tone. "Left bottom without the arm."

Struwe knew the cause right away. The frangibolt holding the 100 kilogram (220 pound) arm had snapped. During the design phase, Struwe had warned against using a single bolt for the arm because it might not be able to support the side to side movement once the arm was extended. Though it wasn't an "I told you so" moment, it was an expensive one: a new arm would cost in the neighborhood of $300,000, and months were needed to make it.

The Triton team went to the deck to recover the sub as the film crew rushed to position their cameras and capture the emotions of Lahey and Vescovo. The sea state had picked up since the launch from a 1 to a 2-plus. It took the LARS team twenty minutes to position the sub behind the ship. Vescovo and Lahey disembarked and returned to the ship in the *Xeno*.

Once in place, the sub was hoisted by the A-frame crane, but it wasn't high enough out of the water when the crane came to a stop. At that precise, inopportune moment, a tailwind whipped through and rocked the sub into the stern of the ship, crushing two thrusters. As the sub bounced off of the ship, Magee, who was running the deck operations, shouted: "Up on the main! Up on main!"

The sub was quickly pulled above the ship,

locked into place and moved onto the ship.

Lahey went down to examine the damage with Magee. The two mangled thrusters would need to be replaced. This in and of itself wasn't a major undertaking, as good planning had assured that there were spares available on the ship. The bigger issue was that a post-dive inspection revealed that a handful of the electrical penetrators into the sub's capsule needed to be replaced, and that was not easily done on the ship. It was a significant issue. In the current condition, the sub couldn't dive.

This new and difficult repair, plus losing the arm, was a totally demoralizing set of events. "It's absolutely heartbreaking," Magee said. "It could be curtains for this trip."

Buckle was becoming increasingly frustrated with Triton's inability to execute the launch and recovery system, and was again bemoaning that there was not a man-rated crane, as he had done when he first saw the ship.

"Patrick always thinks he's right," Buckle said after the disastrous recovery. "You can't tell him what to do. Now we have a launch and recovery system that doesn't work. The fundamentals are flawed. Either the sub is too big for the A-frame, or the A-frame is too small for the sub. You can mitigate the problems but you can't remove the problems, but if we have a new LARS, we can."

The ultimate solution was to install a man-rated

crane. The problems with that were cost and time. The cost would be in the $1 million range, and the time to install it would suspend the expedition, almost certainly causing it to miss the Southern Ocean dive window. Triton would simply have to figure out modifications and process changes to make what they had work. This is what Vescovo did in his day job with factories, and this was a similar problem.

However, Vescovo was also frustrated with the continued series of mechanical issues with the sub, particularly with the problems with the all-important VBT system. "I kept telling them I wanted an M-16 not an AK-47," he said that night at dinner, employing a rifle metaphor. "The M-16 is a better rifle, a precision firearm that is technologically more advanced. The AK-47 is not as accurate, though it also gets the job done."

But while he was slowly losing his patience, he still maintained his sense of humor. "I've joked that this sub cost me an arm and a leg," he added. "Today, it literally cost me an arm." He quickly added that he had no intention of paying for a new one—that since its loss seemed to be a fundamental design flaw, it was Triton's problem to warranty. If they couldn't, he would just do without it and focus on diving, and not potential sample collection.

Lahey had reached a breaking point of sorts. After dinner, he met with his team in the control room. Morale, which had seen its valleys, had crashed like an ill-equipped website. "There was a collective sigh that we had reached the end, that this was not going to happen," he later recalled.

That night, Vescovo, McCallum, Buckle, and Lahey met to discuss what to do next. The schedule could be extended, messing up travel plans heading into Christmas, but that wasn't really the issue. The fact was, there was little evidence that the deep ocean dive could be accomplished with all the problems that had occurred. More than that, it felt like the entire expedition was in jeopardy because the sub couldn't execute a successful dive.

"Have I just wasted $25 million?" Vescovo asked Lahey at one point. "I'm prepared to walk out of here and write it off as a bad debt if there are major design issues that can't be fixed."

"You can't do that," Lahey pleaded. "We can fix it. You've got to give me more time. I need one more day. We can do it."

The group began openly debating the short-term alternatives, either packing it in or giving Triton a day to fix the sub and attempting the deep dive. McCallum gently pushed back, talking about how far the team had come since sea trials. Lahey pleaded for the next day to try and make the sub diveable. He believed in that period of time they could replace the thrusters, reroute electrical connectors through those used by the now-absent manipulator arm, and fix the other issues. Buckle figured there was no downside to at least letting Triton see if they could make the sub ready.

After everyone weighed in, Vescovo said he wanted to think about it.

McCallum then met with Vescovo alone and gave things a hopeful spin. "You can't pull out now," he said. "This has never been done before. We are operating out here without a playbook, without a recipe, without a template. We are learning as we are doing. We are breaking as we are doing. My list of issues from sea trials 'til now has gone from over 100 to 12. But you can't keep leaning on Patrick like that because you are going to give him a stroke and that's not going to help us."

Vescovo, sometimes reasonable to a fault, made the logical decision. Just as he had decided that the team needed to take a risk at the dive off the *Titanic* site to see if the sub could be launched and recovered in rough seas, he had to try for this dive. He remained confident that the absolute *core* systems of the sub—its life support system, pressure hull, and ability to go up and down the water column—had always worked well and had not been compromised by all the failures in the past few days.

"It's a calculated risk, but I've taken greater risks," he said. "This one is reasonable."

He would give the Triton engineers the following thirty-six hours to make the sub diveable, and if accomplished, he would attempt his first solo dive ever on Wednesday to the deepest point of the Atlantic Ocean. Either way, the Puerto Rico Trench mission would end on Thursday, and if that happened without a successful dive, who knew what would happen next with the expedition.

On the morning of the 19th, the sun was radiating off the Atlantic Ocean in a way that made it look like light reflecting off a massive diamond. Overhead, the sky was azure with a slight dusting of clouds visible on the horizon. The sea rippled slightly but was the calmest it had been the entire trip. The conditions to dive were ideal.

After Triton had worked virtually nonstop for thirty-six hours to fix the seeping hatch, replace the damaged thrusters, and repair the VBT system, Lahey deemed the sub ready to go. The big fix was that the conductors freed up by the loss of the manipulator arm allowed Blades to restore full functionality to the other electrical systems—though to make the connections work, there was now a cable running across the back of the two seats.

"We completely rewired the sub," Lahey said. "I don't want to use the term 'hotwired,' but it's ready."

All of the teams gathered for a morning meeting. McCallum started by delivering a pep talk. "We have all worked very long and very hard to get to this point," he said. "It's been a long road . . . the culmination of a dream that's become a reality. In a normal speech, I would call this the moment of truth. But I don't think it's that. I think this is the moment we have been working toward. I would call this the moment of harmony, when all elements come together."

He outlined the dive and detailed the assignments. "We just have to go and execute," he said. "The plan is pretty simple . . ." He paused, gave a heavy laugh, and added, "He says preparing to send a submersible to 8,400 meters under the sea."

He then showed everyone the Explorers Club flag that had been presented to Vescovo in New York. "We are going to add a lot more history to this flag." He folded the flag and handed it to Vescovo. "Take the flag down and bring it back."

"It's like mountaineering," Vescovo said. "It only counts if you come back."

With that, the meeting broke up, and everyone went to prepare for a dive that had been more than three years and tens of millions of dollars in the making.

Vescovo returned to his cabin and packed a bag of items he wanted to take to the bottom of the ocean. For someone who is not sentimental by nature, these were objects that reflected his life. They included the jacket he took to Mount Everest, the North Pole, and the South Pole. He had several folded flags: an American flag given to him when he retired from the Navy reserves, flags of his alma maters—Harvard, Stanford, MIT, and his high school—as well as a UN flag, the Explorers Club flag, and an Albanian one, a tribute to the homeland of his longtime girlfriend, Monika. He also had a Cartier "Love Bracelet" for her, the first of five that he would take down to the bottom of each ocean and then have the coordinates and depth engraved on each one. He had bracelets for his sister Victoria and his step-nieces and two watches, his father's gold Rolex and a silver Rolex his deceased father had given him when he was eighteen. On his actual wrist, however, he wore his new titanium Omega Seamaster Chronometer. He also had the dog collars from his three Schipperkes who had died over the years.

Vescovo zipped his "Go bag" and headed for the launch deck. With Lahey, he walked around the sub and ran through the pre-dive checklist. Finding nothing of concern, he proceeded to the tender to board the *Limiting Factor*.

"Safe dive . . ." Lahey said.

"I'll try," came the reply.

Like clockwork and with precision, the sub was

launched; Vescovo boarded, and the swimmer Quigley sealed the hatch and released the main tow line. All systems in the sub were operational and the control board was green. The dive was a go.

"Life support good," Vescovo reported from inside the *Limiting Factor*. "Starting pumps . . . see you on the other side."

With that, Vescovo began to descend without a copilot for the first time. Lahey had never been crazy about him diving alone, especially not on his first attempt to the bottom. "I'm as nervous as a whore in church," Lahey said.

As the dive progressed uneventfully, everyone in the control room seemed curiously optimistic. Things were going just as they had been drawn up. Vescovo performed his comms checks on the quarter-hour, giving his depth, heading, and indicating that life support was good.

After twenty minutes, he passed through 3,000 meters. An hour into the dive, as he crossed 5,000 meters, he noticed a subtle chirping sound in the capsule. "What the hell is that?" he said to himself. He began cycling circuits and eventually the strange noise stopped.

During this process, he missed a quarter-hour comms check, or at least the control room couldn't hear him. Lahey radioed the ship's bridge to contact the *Learned Response* to come to a stop to prevent any interference.

"Victor . . . can . . . you . . . read . . . me . . ." Lahey said, pausing for a reply. Hearing nothing but static, he hunched over and uttered, "Oh my god . . ."

Lahey reached for a headset and pressed his hands over the ear pieces. Seated next to him, Blades began adjusting knobs on the control board and assured Lahey everything was okay. Almost twenty-five minutes had passed since they had heard from Vescovo.

"Victor, can you read me?" he said slowly. "I say again, can you read me . . . over."

After a full minute of silence, Vescovo's voice came across. "Roger . . . have you good," he said. "I . . . will . . . talk . . . louder."

Lahey ripped off the headset. "Fuckin' A . . ."

McCallum put a hand on his shoulder. "Breathe . . . breathe . . ."

As Vescovo continued his descent, the comms became clearer and depth records began piling up. Reaching 5,000 meters (16,404 feet) made him the second solo pilot to go that deep—only James Cameron in his *Deepsea Challenger* had made a deeper solo dive, to full ocean depth, recorded at 10,908 meters, in 2012. Passing through 6,100 meters (20,013 feet) made the *Limiting Factor* the first American-made submersible to dive deeper than that since the U.S. Navy's DSV-4 *Sea Cliff* in 1985. At 7,100 meters (23,200 feet), it surpassed the world's deepest diving active submersible, China's *Jiaolong*, which had reached 7,020 meters in 2012.

When the *Limiting Factor*'s sonar altimeter indicated that Vescovo was near the bottom, he began looking out the viewport in anticipation. With 200 meters to go to the seafloor, he began to release his small VBT weights to slow the descent and become neutrally buoyant. As designed, the sub slowed as it approached the bottom. At 30 meters, he noticed that the down viewport was actually bringing in more light—the powerful lights of the sub were subtly reflecting off the bottom. Quickly, as the sub closed the last 10 meters, Vescovo could make out what looked like a tan moonscape below him. And then, with barely a sound and imperceptible downward motion, a small puff of silt rose around the *Limiting Factor*.

He had touched bottom.

"Surface, *LF* . . . present depth 8,589 . . . at bottom . . . repeat . . . at bottom," he said, reporting the depth being calculated in decibars.

The control room erupted in cheers. Lahey threw his arms up in the air and made the rounds, high-fiving each one of his team. When converted from decibars to meters, Vescovo had made it down to 8,376 meters (27,480 feet), or 5.2 miles, the bottom of the Puerto Rico Trench, achieving his goal of becoming the first person to reach the absolute nadir of the Atlantic

Ocean at 2:55 P.M. EST on December 19, 2018.

Vescovo piloted the *Limiting Factor* around the bottom to see what could be seen and film the surroundings with the high-definition cameras affixed to the sub. He was struck by the fact there was virtually no current and the brownish sediment on the bottom was barely shifting, creating an elegant geometric pattern of ripples on the seafloor. "I'm at the bottom of the Atlantic Ocean," he said to himself. "It's like I'm on another planet."

With one hand on the joystick to engage the thrusters, he peered out the viewport. "Looks like the surface of the Moon . . ."

Then he spotted an object dead ahead. He piloted in that direction to see what it was. Blackish in color and round in contour, it appeared to be a cracked oil drum wedged into the sediment. He frowned and sighed disgustedly. "Really?" he muttered.

After Vescovo had been roaming around the bottom for forty-five minutes, Lahey began to grow nervous. "We have to stop for safety reasons," he told Blades who was sitting next to him running the electronics—though there was no obvious safety issue.

He radioed Vescovo, recommending that the dive end. Following protocol, Vescovo replied that he agreed and was dropping the surface weight. There was a pause, a sharp "click" in the capsule as Vescovo flipped the weight release switch, and then he was, indeed, ascending. The sub was on its way up.

"Roger that, surface weight dropped, positive ascent," Lahey said into the handheld microphone. "Congratulations."

Lahey clicked off and spun around in his chair. "How about that? You fuckin' guys rock. . . . Now let's get him back on board."

Two and a half hours later, at 6:17 P.M., a burst of light breached the water's surface on the starboard side of the ship, followed by the white top of *Limiting Factor* surfacing to a backdrop of grayish clouds with sunlight streaming through them and lighting the water a surreal shade of aqua.

The LARS team swung into action. Fifteen minutes later, after a flawless and textbook recovery, Vescovo popped out of the sub. "One down!" he yelled, holding up his index finger.

"Victor Vescovo . . . rock star!" shouted Lahey, pumping his fist.

Everyone on the deck applauded. Forty-eight hours after the Five Deeps Expedition appeared to be unraveling, it had achieved its finest moment to date.

That night, a celebratory barbecue was held in the sky bar. Vescovo clutched a bottle of Veuve

Cliquot, drinking directly from the bottle, and detailed his experience of being the first person to ever see the absolute bottom of the Atlantic.

The great irony was that losing the manipulator arm had made the dive successful. The conductors freed up by not having an arm ended up providing Blades a method to fix all of the other electrical faults by rewiring the sub.

"My wife always says, 'Not all bad things come to hurt you,'" Lahey said. "There is something profound about that. We were sitting there facing what looked like an absolute failure when the arm dropped off, but that was what made it possible for Victor to have that dive."

Lahey also pointed out that pushing for the extra time to fix the sub when it looked like all was lost had saved the entire trip. "People criticize my optimism, but Victor was ready to throw his toys out of the crib," Lahey said. "It was my fucking relentless optimism that pushed us through and got that dive done."

There was also talk of what had been discovered by the science team, though the footage from Atlantic's cameras had not been fully reviewed. Science had taken a back seat to the core mission—to dive to the bottom—but at least four new species of sea creatures had been discovered, and they could be used as a benchmark in the ongoing examination of biodiversity at full ocean depth. On the geological side, Stewart had identified "slumps" in the trench on the sonar scans, small depressions that could trigger a tsunami as they expanded, data that she would turn over to local geologists in hopes of furthering their understanding of their undersea environment. "Baby steps, but a start," Stewart said.

As the champagne flowed, an emotional and spent Lahey stood to present Vescovo with a submersible test pilot certificate. "I've trained a lot of sub pilots in my life, been doing this thirty years," he said. "Never have I had a trainee who has had to endure so many problems over the course of a dozen dives. It has been truly surprising, unnerving, disappointing, but at the same time pretty remarkable. It has been an opportunity to test you in ways that maybe you hadn't expected."

Vescovo took the certificate and hugged Lahey.

"Today, you really stole the show," Lahey continued. "I think everybody on the ship thought, Holy shit man, this guy has balls of fucking steel . . ."

Over the laughter, someone shouted, "Titanium!"

Vescovo stood and raised his champagne bottle. "Thank you, Triton," he said. "Thank you . . . you guys made it happen."

There was still a long, long way to go to

complete the next four ocean dives, but in one single, record-breaking dive, it felt like the entire expedition had turned a corner, that possibility was heading toward reality.

Worldwide Deep Submergence Vehicles (As of September 1, 2020)

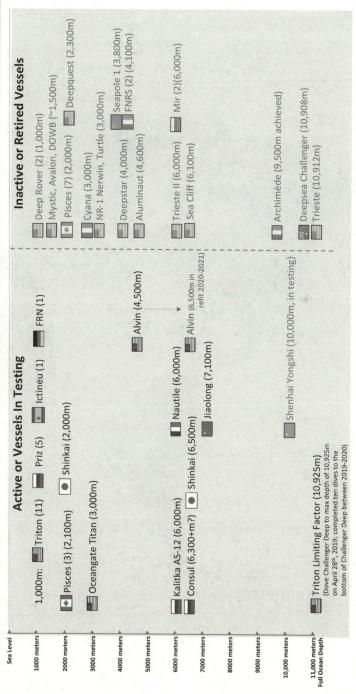

A Snapshot of the History of the World's Deep Ocean Submersibles. *Credit: Caladan Oceanic.*

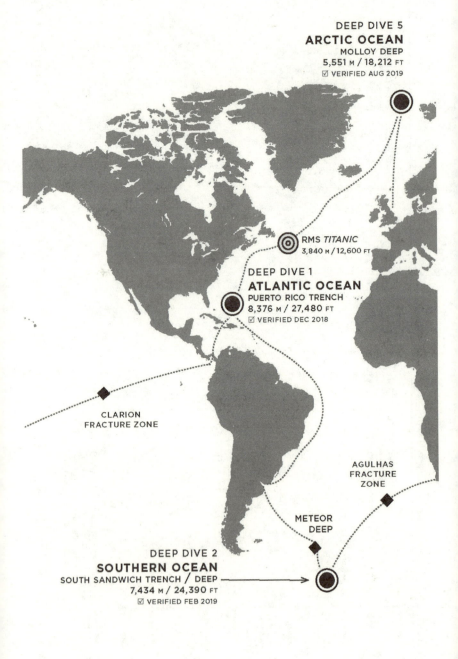

DEEP DIVE 5
ARCTIC OCEAN
MOLLOY DEEP
5,551 M / 18,212 FT
☑ VERIFIED AUG 2019

◎ RMS *TITANIC*
3,840 M / 12,600 FT

DEEP DIVE 1
ATLANTIC OCEAN
PUERTO RICO TRENCH
8,376 M / 27,480 FT
☑ VERIFIED DEC 2018

CLARION
FRACTURE ZONE

AGULHAS
FRACTURE
ZONE

METEOR
DEEP

DEEP DIVE 2
SOUTHERN OCEAN
SOUTH SANDWICH TRENCH / DEEP ⟶
7,434 M / 24,390 FT
☑ VERIFIED FEB 2019

THE FIVE DEEPS EXPEDITION

ATLANTIC · SOUTHERN · INDIAN · PACIFIC · ARCTIC

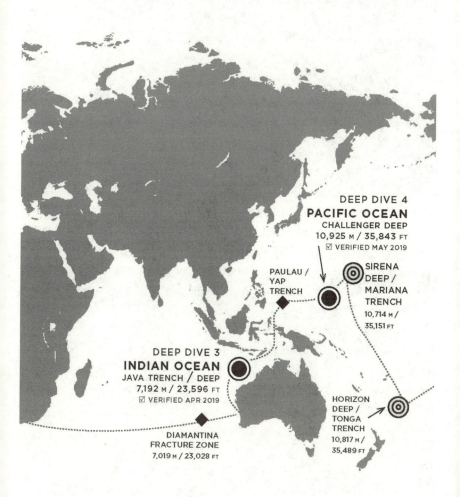

DEEP DIVE 4
PACIFIC OCEAN
CHALLENGER DEEP
10,925 M / 35,843 FT
☑ VERIFIED MAY 2019

PAULAU /
YAP
TRENCH

SIRENA
DEEP /
MARIANA
TRENCH
10,714 M /
35,151 FT

DEEP DIVE 3
INDIAN OCEAN
JAVA TRENCH / DEEP
7,192 M / 23,596 FT
☑ VERIFIED APR 2019

HORIZON
DEEP /
TONGA
TRENCH
10,817 M /
35,489 FT

DIAMANTINA
FRACTURE ZONE
7,019 M / 23,028 FT

● PRIMARY "DEEP" DIVES ◎ SUPPLEMENTAL DIVES ◆ SONAR & MAPPING OPERATIONS